THRESHOLD

CRAIG TEMPLE

Contents

Preface

The name Tobias is Greek for God's goodness and Threshold means the limit or capacity. The question is what is the limit of God's goodness? Has he or she let evil control the world that we live in or is there a plan to rid this world of these demons? Everyday there are events and actions that go on that are good and some that are evil. That just lets us know that there is a never ending power struggle between both sides. Some people see good as evil and evil as good. Who is right and who is wrong? Can the people that we see as doing good be the ones that are doing the most harm to the world?

As a child, I grew up wanting to be like the heroes I've seen in comics and television. As an adult I see that most of the villains are also heroes but they do things differently. Just because someone has different views than you don't make them a bad person. Man cannot beat a monster alone. Maybe it takes a monster to beat a monster and God is the only one that knows that. Maybe the monster that we need is just that one person you see everyday and you don't know it. There are so many people in this world and many new creatures being discovered every day. Have you ever stopped to ask where they came from and how they got here?

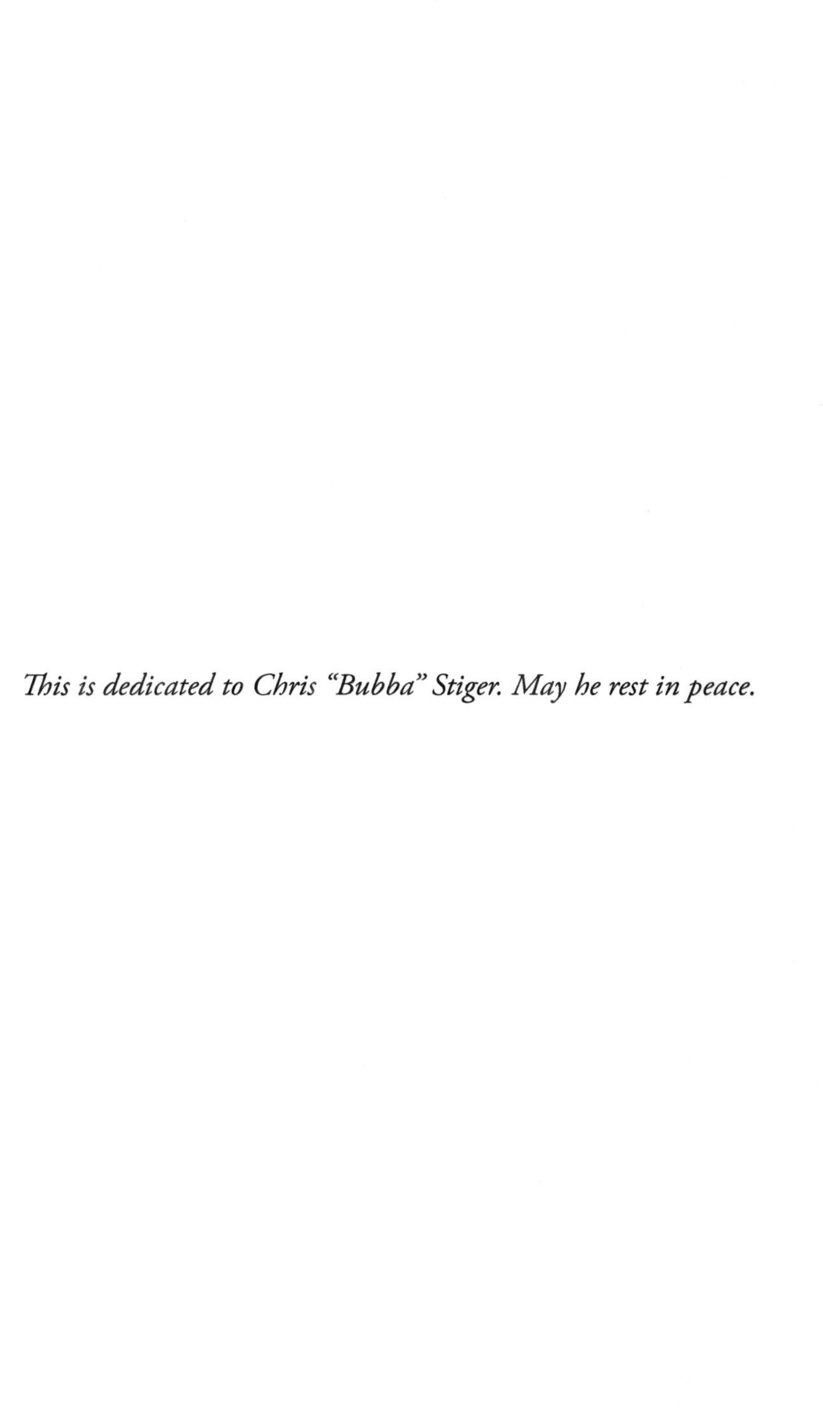

This is dedicated to Chris "Bubba" Stiger. May he rest in peace.

Acknowledgements

There are a few people I want to thank for helping me on this adventure. First and foremost, Chris "Bubba" Stiger. If it wasn't for you turning me onto a lot of conspiracy theories I wouldn't have anything to write about. Brian Kitchen for helping me learn and grow as an author and for pointing out my mistakes so I can finish out the final draft. Yes the young and talented artist Martina thank you for the illustrations. What's an adventure without picking up some friends on the way. I'm looking forward to chilling on the beaches of Croatia with you in the future. My family for all their moral support. Mom, Dad love you guys. Aunt Carol helped me out a lot in life. Thanks for being my cheerleaders. Also I will have to give the biggest thanks to Tara Carson of URLink Publishing. Without her words of encouragement for Threshold I would have put it on the shelf a while ago. I have the same hopes and expectations as you do. Last but not least, I have to thank all the haters that have told me not to go the route I chose. Haven't you learned by now. Don't take advice from fools. Thank you all.

Prologue

The cool winds howled carrying with them fresh snow to the land of Pixima. King Edward Moranvale watched the snow swirl through the air, his face lackluster as he watched the castle grounds slowly disappear around Branville. Sighing, he climbed into his bed and crawled under the covers, but found quickly that he was unable to sleep. Turning his gaze towards the window once again, he watched the snow swirling in the wind in the deep purple sky. Scowling, he drew the blanket over his head and turned away from the window, but still his worries continue to persist. Much like the snow his people's opinion of him was falling. They lost faith in the king that slept safe in the comfort of his castle, warm and well fed, while they struggled to provide enough food for their families. He knew if something did not change soon his rule will be at an end.

Why should a king give up his wealth for a peasant? There has to be a way to change their image of me. To see me as a valiant king and not as a tyrant. With those thoughts in mind, he decided to get out of his bed to speak with the royal oracle. Still in his sleeping gown and cap he picks up his bedside torch. Setting out for the trek down the spiral staircase that lead to the basement. Lifting a hand he moved to knock, but stopped short as the door creaked open.

"Come in my lord. I've been expecting you," a voice called from the shadows.

Stepping into the room he asked, "I trust you know why I'm here old woman?" The oracle nodded before lowering the hood of her robe exposing her pale, weathered face to the candle light.

"You seek to know the future, but the future is based on choices. Every choice has a consequence," she replied. Walking over to peer her blank eyes into the cauldron in the center of the room. "The cauldron says that choice one leads to the strongest era of Pixima. A striped one shall lead the country to greatness IF you step down from power."

"Is there another option?" he questioned her. She turned to him with her lifeless eyes and brown brittle teeth.

"It is said that a deal of darkness will be made. War will be waged. Death will fill the land. New worlds will be discovered leading to dual power, but beware the one that dwells amongst the trees."

In his tired response he stated, "So be it. I will take the second option." The oracle smiled and took the king by the hand.

"A drop of blood and the deal will be done," she cackled. Using a small dagger to slice his hand. As the blood trickled into the cauldron the oracle laughed. "Let the Demon Wars commence!" Shadows risen from the bubbling liquid and circled the room as she danced and laughed.

The shadows whispered, "You made your choice now deal with it." Circling King Edward, the winds ruffling his gown. "Death, death, death to the first born sons." Then they left up the stairwell, all but one.

"What does it ask of me?" inquired King Edward.

The oracle responded, "Offerings. The souls of the damned." Heeding her words from before, "Beware the one that dwells amongst the trees."

"I offer the souls of the jungle beasts!" he yelled out. "The ones that dwell amongst the trees!"

Waking in his bed, like it was all just a dream, King Edward peers out his window to gaze among the snow-covered trees. All of them full of hanging bodies above the blood drenched snow. Boys of the age of thirteen and under, except one woman with child right outside his bedroom window. He knew what he has done. Now he knows what needed to be done. War upon the demons...

SEASON I

DIRTY DEEDS

It was a nice sunny day in the small town of Branville, the capital of Pixima. There was a warm spring breeze blowing the scent of freshly grilled meat through the trees. The sounds of festival music and the murmur of the crowd filled the air. Marshall Badgon was patrolling the streets to ensure the safety of King Edward Moranvale's arrival for the celebration of their victory in the Demon Wars.

"Good day, all seems well here," he smirked at a group of ladies passing. Turning their heads slightly they smiled and giggled, admiring his short black hair and beard.

"Marshal, what are you doing!?" said Captain Salles. Grabbing his attention, "We are here to make sure the king is safe. Not to satisfy your urges," he scolded him. "The Demon Wars may be over, but you never know what troubles roam these streets."

"I'm sorry sir," he apologized. "Sometimes I can't help myself. It's in my nature." he grinned.

"I get the gist of that, but with all seriousness. The war might be over but you never know who or what can be out there that wants the head of the king!" reprimanded Captain Salles. "Now get back out there and do your duty!"

Marshall Badgon stood up straight and saluted, "Yes sir! I will sir!" He then hurried passed all the festivities, looking for anything out of the ordinary. He passed through the large noisy crowd of masked dancers and patrons. He ignored the smells of fresh vegetables and meat as he passed the vendors. There was one thing he failed to notice before reporting back to Captain Salles though. He bypassed a suspicious man in a red hooded cloak at a vendor in the far corner by the trees.

"It is safe sir," he panted. "All is well in Branville." He bent over with his hands on his knees, out of breath.

"Good, the king is ready to address the people," stated Captain Salles. The tall blonde man turned to face the balcony of Branville castle. The crowd roared at the sight of King Edward Moranvale.

"My people!" spoke the old white haired man. He raised his hand to silence the noisy crowd. "This celebration is in honor of the troops! The ones that have lived and those who have sacrificed themselves to send the demons back to the underworld!" The crowd cheered in approval of the king's words. King Moranvale continued to speak as the man in the red hood began pushing his way to the front of the crowd. He picked the pockets of the guests for just mere change. Silencing the crowd again, "I try to be a peaceful old bird, but we also have to do what we must to ensure the safety of the people of this land!"

"The safety?!" King Moranvale heard. The Irish accent came from the front of the crowd. "All the troops were out everywhere except the Jungles of Pixima. Why was that, sire?" questioned the red hooded man.

"I have chosen to protect the ones that are worth the cause!" Moranvale replied. "The ones that live in the jungle are nothing but murderous thieves that should be able to protect themselves! That's if they want to live!" He laughed in the face of the angered man. The man then took off his hood to reveal his long red hair and red beard.

"I am Tobias Threshold of the Jungles of Pixima!" he stated angrily. "I have watched my wife and two children brutally murdered by the shadows of the night!" He walked closer to the balcony where Moranvale stood. "I watched as my own son ripped his mother's gut opened and pulled out her intestines! Then he turned to his sister and grabs her by the hair! I heard her screams of agony as he pulled until her head came off! Then all I could do was watch as he turned to me and smiled! Right before he ripped out his own throat, spewing his blood at my feet!" The crowd looked on in horror at his words. "I have done what I could to protect them! I have failed them! My Lord, we are mere people too! You cannot blame the people of the jungle for what we have become! It is the society that you swore to protect that has oppressed us to become outcasts!" Moranvale paced back and forth on the balcony rubbing his chin in confusion.

"Well, Mr. Threshold, that does seem to be a tragedy, but pointing fingers at me for you being a mere low life criminal makes no sense. None at all," Moranvale responded.

Captain Salles turned to Marshall Badgon and stated, "I thought you said all is well? What the fuck, Marshall? Were you thinking with the wrong head again?" They made their way closer to where Threshold was, but they were too late. They heard a loud angry roar that frightened the crowd. Everyone scattered to take cover. Where the red haired man once stood was a seven foot tall lion beast. His rippling muscles covered in short reddish brown fur and his long red mane blowing in the breeze. The two guards looked up towards the king. He too began to change. Dropping his white robe, brown feathers grew upon his arms, his nose and mouth slowly came together to form an eagle's beak and his white hair changed to white feathers.

It was a rare occurrence that the people of Branville got to see the eagle king. This time was for his own protection as the enraged lion beast leaped towards the balcony. Moranvale soared into the sky. Before Threshold could make it to the balcony a large black and white tiger met him in the sky with a thud. They crashed to the ground in front of Captain Salles in his bengal tiger form. They circled around the would be assassin in the empty grass field. The festival goers looked on from the safety of the surrounding buildings and trees. Badgon tries a diving bite for the back of Threshold's neck and Salles goes for the legs to subdue the large lion. Salles slides under Threshold as he did a leaping turn to claw Badgon's face. After getting knocked down, Badgon stood up fully on his back legs. Furious at his own failure, he came back with two claw swipes to Threshold's chest. Both of them now streaming in blood, Badgon's face and Threshold's chest. Before Salles could jump in, the eagle king managed to swoop in and knock Threshold down. Badgon and Moranvale pinned him down until he changed back to his human form. Salles then cuffed and pulled the poor beaten Threshold to his feet. He slowly escorted him towards the dungeon on the back side of the castle.

"This isn't over!" Threshold screamed and struggled. "I speak for the survivors of the Jungles of Pixima!"

Stopping for a second Salles asked, "How many survived?"

He replied, "Just one, me."

Threshold heard footsteps on the cold stone floor. He looked up from the dark corner of his cell to see the old face of King Moranvale staring down at him. He had nothing to say to the old man. Only a look of anger and disgust from the darkness he sat in.

"Oh poor Threshold. So lost and alone in this cruel world," Moranvale mocked him. "What will he ever do? Guard, leave us to speak alone." Marshal Badgon salutes the king and turns to walk down the long dark hallway. As soon as the dungeon door closed five shadows appeared around Moranvale. "Yes, Threshold, they are with me," Moranvale laughed. "You see, the real reason the Jungles were destroyed was to protect my throne. All of this was orchestrated by me." He paced back and forth in front of the cell. "There were allegations of treason and word of me being stripped of my throne. I had to do something to show my true power, so I made a deal with the underworld council." Threshold stood up from the cold stone floor.

"What's the point of telling me this?" he asked. "I'm still alive and the law states all are due to a fair trial."

Rubbing his chin and laughing, Moranvale replied, "Yes that is true. Too bad you won't be alive for long. I just wanted you to know why your family had to die." He continued to pace as he began to explain. "You see, in order to receive the services of the council I had to offer the souls of the damned. Since you lions were nothing but the scourge of society. There was no better payment for my reputation." He stopped pacing and stared at Threshold. "Don't worry though. You will be reunited with your family soon." He turned and walked away. "Give it some time and make it look like a suicide." The shadows nodded in acknowledgement. Badgon sensed something bad in the air, so he was hiding in the darkness of an open cell. He heard the whole thing and decided to free Threshold. He fumbled with the keys nervously.

"You need to run or they will kill you. I will tell Captain Salles everything I heard here," he stammered.

"You need to hurry or they will kill us both," Threshold replied. Badgon finally got the door unlocked.

"They are just shadows. They cannot harm us without a host body," he answered.

"That's why you are here," whispered a faint voice. The keys fell from Badgon's hand and his body quivered. His eyes changed black as the midnight sky. The voice now spoke through Badgon. "So this is what it's like to be a Lycan," laughed the demon. He picked Threshold up by the throat. "If I can do this in human form imagine the possibilities if I fully change."

Threshold didn't give him that chance. He swung his legs back to get power for a kick to the abdomen. After crashing to the floor Threshold jumps up with a hard uppercut. Knocking the possessed Badgon to the ground, he ran down the long dark hallway of the dungeon.

"After him! I want him dead!" yelled the possessed Badgon. The other four shadows flown down the hallway and pursued him through the moonlit streets. Badgon changes to the tiger beast and joins the pursuit, heading towards the Jungles of Pixima. The others branched off to find hosts of their own.

Threshold ran through the mass of bodies and blood of his fallen kind. He stopped to see the remains of his loving family before heading further into the jungle. The memories flowed in as he looked in horror at their battered bodies. Memories of his wife's long blonde hair flowing in the wind while she hung clothes out to dry. Images of his ginger haired daughter chasing his son around the yard at the same time. "You will never catch me!" the boy laughed as the memories faded away.

"I knew you would come here," said a voice from behind him. He turned around to see Badgon standing there in his white tiger form. The others showed up one by one after his arrival. First to show was a tall, slender, blonde woman followed by a clean shaven muscular man with short black hair. Then a shorter elderly gentleman showed followed by a tiny dwarf.

"Sorry sir," the dwarf apologized. "Looks like these two got the good ones. Not that much to choose from this time of night."

Threshold looks back at the group of misfits and quotes his son's words. "You will never catch me," he said as he disappeared into the darkness. Running through the hot jungle he felt a sudden icy wind blowing, sending a chill throughout his body. He pulled up his hood to try to subdue the freezing pain. He pushed forth fore it meant either life or death. A foul stench of rotting flesh forced him to stop deep in the uncharted area. Following the rancid smell, he came across a large metal machine with wings like a bird. "Is this some sort of flying machine?" he thought out loud examining it.

"Well, well. Like the saying goes. Curiosity killed the cat," laughed a womanly voice. He turned around to look upon the tall beautiful woman.

"Who are you?" he asked.

"I am your death," she replied.

"No! Who were you before the demon got your soul!" he demanded to know.

"Just a mere bar wench!" she answered drawing her sword. The sword flew out of her hand and stuck to a large rock near the flying machine.

"Looks like the fates are on my side," he stated. He pulls his hood back up and walk toward the origin of the icy winds. "'Till we meet again wench," as he disappeared into the mist.

"Ahhh!" he screamed. Splashing down in a large river in the midst of the night. Lost and confused, he swam to the shore. Soaking wet, he walked away from the river. The place he was in was filled with strange buildings, paved roads and monuments of people he never seen before. Standing next to a Potomac River sign he asked himself, "Where the hell am I?"

THE NEW WORLD

The wench ran back through the dark jungle to let, what used to be Marshal Badgon, know what has happened. She found him standing in front of the Threshold home basking in the stench of death.

"Damn it, Alastor! I had him cornered but he got away," she panted heavily. "We have to report this to Moranvale."

Angered by her statement, "That's great, Lilith!" he replied. "How did he get away?! Did he just disappear!?"

"Something like that," replied Lilith. "Was a strange area. Cold winds, magnetic rocks and some strange flying machine. If you don't believe me I can show you. He followed her deep into the uncharted regions of the jungle running as fast as they could. They finally came to the point of Threshold's disappearance.

Examining the wrecked aircraft Alastor asked, "So this is the strange flying machine you referred to?"

"Yes it is," Lilith replied.

Pointing at the sword, "And this is the wench's blade stuck to it?" he questioned.

"Yea. As soon as I pulled it out a strong force pulled it away from me," she answered. Alastor walked slowly examining the aircraft.

"You said he went off in this direction?" he questioned. He looked around for any traps he might have fallen into. He sensed something odd in the cold windy air. He stuck his hand into the mist in front of him only to see it vanish from sight. He pulled his hand back astonished. "There is a nothingness here!" he exclaimed. Out of curiosity, he decided to put his head into the nothingness to look. Alastor pulled his head back out and turned to Lilith. "There is something there, a whole nother world. We have to report this to Moranvale.

"Get out of the road, freak! People are trying to drive here!" Threshold heard. Followed by a loud honking sound. He then heard someone else yell, "Hey weirdo! The renaissance fair isn't 'til this summer!" Threshold was still confused about where he was. Panicking he darted out of the road and down a dark alley. Exhausted and disoriented he squats down next to a trash bin and closes his eyes. A small boy walked up to him as he sat there with his eyes closed.

"Daddy. I have found you," the boy whispered. Threshold opens his eyes to see his son standing before him.

"Xavier! You're alive!" he screamed in excitement.

"No father, I am not,"Xavier responded. The boy's face turned pale and blood ran down from where his throat was. Threshold stood up and backed into the trash bin from fright. "They are coming father. The demons are coming."

"Coming for you?" stuttered Threshold.

"No, coming for the new world. Open your mind and let me show you," Xavier said. He held his lifeless hands out and touched his face. Images came flooding in to Threshold's mind. Images of bodies burning. Images of men and women in suits with pitch black eyes. "This is the New World Order," they spoke. He also heard cries of help from battered and bloody bodies lying in a grove. The cries were settled to the sound of one woman's voice. The woman's cries for help startled him awake. He jumped to his feet and ran towards the screams. His nightmare still fresh in his head.

He walked up on three brown skinned men. They were holding down a short woman with shoulder length brown hair. Her shirt was torn revealing half of a black undergarment. Her jeans were torn off and thrown by the alley wall. One man was holding her down by the shoulders and the other held her legs open. The other was undoing his pants to have his way with her.

"Let her go and walk away," Threshold demanded. He scowled at the rapists. The men looked to see who it was. The one that was standing started to approach Threshold.

"What? Did you just get off the boat, Irish boy?" he laughed.

"I said let her go and walk away," he demanded again.

"Or else what?" the young thug asked. He continued to walk towards Threshold.

"Now that depends on what you are," Threshold replied. He removed his red cloak and dropped it to the ground. The Hispanic man turned to look at the other two. They were still holding the battered woman on the ground.

"Hey! Irish here wants to know who we are!" he laughed. "We are the Latino Saints. Welcome to D.C., Irish." He pulled out a knife and lunged at Threshold. Dodging out of the way, he lets out a blood curdling roar. The thug was stunned for a moment but showed no fear. He continued to attack Threshold with frantic slashes and thrusts of the small blade. He decided to show them what he was. Threshold began to undergo his change. He grew taller, reddish tan fur covered his body and his long red hair formed into his lion's mane.

"Enough!" he roared. The men stopped and stared in fear at the beast before them.

"W-w-what the hell is that?" stuttered the leader. They ran out of the alley into the night. The young woman looked up at him as he changed back to his human form.

"Where is the nearest village?" he asked. "We must get you help." She smiled at him and fainted from exhaustion.

Back in the throne room at Branville Castle, Moranvale and Alastor were speaking.

"You are telling me there is an entrance to a new world in the jungle?" asked Moranvale. He rubbed his chin sitting back in his throne.

"I didn't believe Lilith neither until she showed me," Alastor replied. "We think that's where he disappeared. We must send a scout to search, but who?"

"Send Salles. He is expendable," Moranvale replied.

FRIEND OR FOE

Salles just entered the castle when he was summoned to the throne room. He followed the servant to the brightly lit room. He approached Moranvale and dropped down on one knee.

"You beckoned, sire," he stated.

"It has come to my attention that the prisoner, Threshold, has escaped," Moranvale replied. "The marshall was on guard at the time. He told me he took chase deep into the jungle when he lost him. I need you to track him down."

"I'm going to need some scouts, sir," Salles replied. "I will need Badgon to assist me too." Moranvale sat back in his throne.

"The marshall will not be able to make the trip," he answered. "It seems he was severely injured during the chase. I will be able to send the Marsters with you to assist."

"They will do just fine, sir," Salles replied. "We shall leave as soon as possible." Salles had a gut feeling something wasn't right, but he did not question his king. He turned and walked out of the throne room to gather the Marsters brothers. The Marsters were three elite hunters. They can track down who or what needed to be found just on smell alone. They were also the strongest of all the warriors in Pixima. Far from the brightest though. He knew right where to find them. He headed out of the castle and down the dirt road to the Wolves Den Tavern. He walked through the swinging doors and immediately seen them sitting at the bar. He approached them as to not alert the patrons.

He leaned in and whispered, "The king has a job for you." The oldest brother, Ranger, turned and gave Salles a stern look then chugged his mead.

"What kind of job is it?" he grumbled.

"The prisoner has escaped and Moranvale wants him tracked down," Salles replied. "Your job is to find him, mine is to bring him in. I'm sure you will be properly compensated."

"Hey boys, looks like the king needs us to catch a cat!" laughed Ranger. "Y'all think we should take it?"

"You better," replied the tavern owner. He took Ranger's empty stein and wiped the counter. "All this mead isn't gonna pay for itself." Ranger looked towards his brothers, Butch and Spike.

"Okay, count us in. The pay better be good," he answered Salles. He looked at the bartender and asked, "Where is the usual wench today anyways?"

"Don't know. She never showed for her shift," he replied. "Things have been a little peculiar since after the festival though."

"Yes they have been," commented Salles. He stood up off his stool to leave. "Take some time for preparations and meet me in front of Branville Castle at sundown. I'll be waiting there," he told the brothers. He then left through the same swinging doors he entered.

The sun was setting when the Marsters approached the castle. The moon lit up the incoming darkness.

"Good, you all came. Shall we proceed with this endeavor?" Salles asked. He started to head off towards the jungle.

"When will we get paid?" Butch asked.

"The king said when the job is done, everyone will be compensated," replied Salles.

"Well boys, let's just make this quick then," commented Ranger. They followed Salles into the moonlit jungle. They ventured about a mile into the trees when they came across the bloody massacre that was the lion race.

"That smell. Why has no one cleaned this up?" asked Spike from the back of the pack.

"Because no one cared enough to come back here," Butch replied. They marched on through the bloody scene and stench of decay until they came upon the Threshold home. Salles went inside to inspect the house. The table was still set with plates at all four seats. A loaf of, what was, fresh baked bread in the middle. The stench of rotting flesh filled the air as Salles looked around for clues. The Marsters separated to check the other rooms.

"This must be his wife!" Butch yelled so the others could hear him. Salles came running to the room to see. He hovered over the body of the disemboweled woman lying on the floor. Across the room was the head of a small girl next to the body of a young boy. A bloody hole in his neck where his throat used to be. A smile on his face and a clump of the girl's hair in his hand. They looked on at the horrific display.

"Only a demon could be this heartless as to do something like this," Salles stated. "We seen what we came to see. Now we must move on." He turned and headed to the exit of the home. Upon leaving they all failed to notice a big black bird peering down on them through the darkness.

"The scent leads this way, sir," Spike said. Pointing forward from the back of the pack. "There is also an unfamiliar smell coming from that direction." They trudged on through the freezing winds blowing.

"There is no way he could have survived this long in this weather!" exclaimed Ranger.

"Just be on your guard!" Salles yelled back. "We do not know what dwells in these parts!" Bracing the wind, they kept moving until Salles came to a sudden stop. "What is this?" he asked. He walked around the big metal machine staring in wonder. "I've never seen anything like it before." Not paying attention to his surroundings, Salles tripped over a big rock. He stumbled backwards falling into the nothingness of the unforeseen void. Out of curiosity Butch and Ranger walked up to where Salles tripped at to see where he went. Spike stayed back by the flying machine to let his older brothers look. He heard the loud thud of the giant black bird on the top of the metal. The sound startled him sending him running towards his brothers. He collided with them forcing them into the same void Salles fell into. Splashing down into the same river Threshold did the day before.

"Damn it! Where the hell are we?" exclaimed Salles.

"I'm not sure, sir, but it's a great night for a swim. Don't you think," Spike laughed. Ranger just grabbed him by the hood of his green cloak and pulled him out of the water.

Out of anger Salles yelled, "Come on you morons! We have work to do!"

"Ms. Buxton, your tests say you are going to be okay," said the emergency room doctor. "You are lucky the man who saved you came along when he did."

"Actually it's Dr. Buxton. I'm a physicist for the Pentagon," she replied. She sat up in the hospital bed. "By the way, have you seen my hero? I think he was wearing a red hooded robe. Strange man." The doctor sat his clipboard on the counter and looked at her.

"I can't say that I have," he replied. "All I know is that he carried you in here and said that you needed help. He just vanished after that. Someone like that shouldn't be that hard to find around here though." He reached into a cabinet below the counter and pulled out a bag of clothes. "I know the clothes you shown up in were torn apart, so one of the nurses donated some you could have." He sat them on the counter. "You are free to go now. Good luck on finding your hero." He walked towards the door to leave.

"Yea, hopefully I can. I owe him a debt of gratitude," she responded. She got up to grab the bag of clothes as he shut the door behind him. After she got dressed Buxton went to the front desk to check out.

"Everything is good ma'am. You are good to leave," the receptionist told her. "Your insurance should cover your stay."

"It better. The outrageous prices I pay a month for it," Buxton replied.

"Only in America," laughed the receptionist.

"Yea, seems like it," commented Buxton. "Now I have to go find the guy who saved my life." The automatic doors opened for her to leave.

"I wish some handsome man will save me," the receptionist said to herself.

Threshold went back to the alley where he saved Buxton. It wasn't too far from the hospital where he took her. It was the only dark place he knew he could hide. He squatted down next to the trash bin again. He still felt lost and confused. He heard footsteps coming up the alley.

"Hello," he heard a woman's voice. "You aren't from around here are you?" she asked. He looked up from underneath his hood just to see the same short brown haired woman he saved the day before.

"No," he replied. "And it's not safe to be around me." He looked back down at the ground.

"What's your name and where are you from?" Buxton asked.

"Don't think you want to know me," he glared at her. "Just know that it's not safe here. You should leave." Captain Salles and the Marsters brothers entered the alley.

"Tobias Threshold! I know you are here! Come out and turn yourself in!" yelled Salles. The sound echoed in the dark alley as he walked down it. "King Moranvale sent us to collect you!"

"Run now," Threshold told her. "This is gonna get a little hairy." She ran out of the alley as fast as she could. Threshold stood up and yelled, "Salles! I am here! Took you long enough to find me!" He stepped out of the shadows.

"I don't want to fight you, Tobias. I just want to hear your side of the story," Salles replied.

"Is that right," he answered. He stared Salles down. "I'm just a common criminal. What makes you think I'm believable?" The Marsters began to circle around Threshold.

"Stand down," Salles told the Marsters. "I feel there is something odd about all this and I don't like it," he told Threshold. "I need to hear what you have to say. Damn it! I said stand down!" They continued to surround Threshold, ready to pounce.

"And I say I need this bounty. We have a tab to pay," Ranger responded.

"Guys, maybe we should listen to the captain," said Spike. He started to back away from Threshold.

"Damn it Spike! You always follow orders and never think for yourself!" complained Butch.

"Not true. You just never take time to listen to me," Spike replied. His words fell on deaf ears as the brothers pounced on Threshold. Spike and Salles tried to pull them off but it was too late. A loud roar echoed through the alley as Threshold threw them off. Ranger and Butch both crashed head first into the brick wall. Spike was thrown against the dumpster and Salles rolled out of the way.

Standing back up, Salles said, "Calm down Tobias. I just want to talk. They just didn't want to listen." He backed away with his hands in the air to show no harm.

"You want to talk. Well answer me this. Where is Badgon?" growled Threshold. He stalked Salles like he was prey.

"I was told he was injured in your escape," Salles answered.

"Lies! You were told nothing but lies!" he yelled. Salles felt threatened. He started to change, showing his stripes.

"Then tell me the truth!" he yelled back. They didn't realize that they were being watched as they circled each other. The large black bird from the jungle perched on the roof top. Buxton peered from around the corner of the alley.

"Everything is a lie. Badgon let me out," answered Threshold.

"Why would he do that?" Salles asked. "He had his orders."

"Moranvale is working with the demons," he answered. "The marshall was taken over by demons." He seen Buxton looking on from her hiding place. "I told you to run and leave me be!" he scolded her. She came out and walked towards them.

"I thought I was dreaming but this is all too real. Who are you? What are you?" she asked. Her curiosity was getting the best of her. They ignored her questions.

"Were you followed here?" Threshold asked Salles.

"No. Why?" Salles replied. Threshold pointed towards the roof. He looked up to see the tall blonde bar wench standing there. She looked down upon them and laughed.

"Yes, and there seems to be only one way in and no way out for you!" she exclaimed. She morphed back to her bird form and flew off towards the river entrance.

"I really have no clue what is going on here, but you helped me so I want to help you," stated Buxton. "By the way, I'm Michelle Buxton and you are?"

"I'm Tobias Threshold of the Jungles of Pixima," replied Threshold.

"I'm Indigo Salles from Branville," Salles responded.

"Indigo?" Threshold smirked.

"This doesn't mean we are friends," scowled Salles. "We can finish this later. Let's go before the Marsters wake up." Transforming back to his human form he grabbed his brown cloak and put it on. Threshold also changed back and puts his cloak back on. "Okay, Michelle Buxton. How do you propose to help us?" he asked.

"I'll figure it out when you tell me the whole story," she answered. "First you guys need a makeover. That's if you want

to fit in around here." They both looked at each other confused. Then they looked back at Buxton. "Let's just head back to my place and figure it out from there," she said. They all walked out of the dark alley to head to Buxton's apartment.

THE MAKEOVER

Lilith met up with Alastor at the entrance to Branville Castle to give her report. Upon her arrival they walked inside to meet with Moranvale.

"Salles has left with Threshold and some strange woman," she told Alastor. "They left the Marsters lying unconscious in the street." They began to ascend the spiral stairs to the throne room.

"How does he know he can trust him?" Alastor asked.

"I don't think he truly does yet. He might just be going off instinct," Lilith replied.

"Let him trust his guts for now. Soon he won't have any to trust," Alastor growled. "Were you seen?" he inquired.

"Yea, but there is no way for them to get back. They are trapped," she answered. "The only way back is high above a river. Only flyers can get there." They stopped at the top of the stairs. Alastor got a sinister look towards Lilith.

"So they are stuck there?" he asked. "Tell me about this new world." Lilith leaned back against the wall and crossed her arms.

"From what I have seen it's a very strange place," she sighed. "All the buildings are made of stone and glass like castles. The beings there all dress in odd attire. There are also machines they use to travel in. Some larger than others. The technology far surpasses ours."

"Yes. I see," he responded. Alastor stroked his beard in thought. "All is going to what the oracle has told. We have to get the other three out of those bodies and send them to the wolves. That lion must die." He opened the door to the throne room and approached Moranvale. He kneeled down before him. "Sire, the new world has been discovered."

"That was an interesting story," Buxton said. She walked with Threshold and Salles down the crowded streets of Washington D.C. She borrowed a couple of lab coats for them to use until they got their own clothes. "That just confirms my Bermuda Triangle Theory of interdimensional travel. That thing you called a flying machine is most likely the fighter jet that went missing last year during a drill."

"What is interdimensional travel and where are we going?" asked Salles. Threshold was not too far behind not paying attention. He watched all the different people walking the busy streets.

"Other scientists think there is a Multiverse out there that we can't get too," she replied. "You know, multiple universes that hold multiple possibilities. Well I have a theory based on the disappearances in the Bermuda Triangle throughout history." She stopped and looked at Threshold and Salles to explain her theory. "I think that if there is a strong magnetic pole where a high pressure system and low pressure system collide a gateway to another dimension will open." Threshold looked at Salles.

"I have no idea what she is talking about," he stated.

"And this is where we are going," Buxton said. She opened the door to a large building. "It's called a mall. Here you can find all you need to fit in this world." She held the door open for them to go through. They looked at all the shops in amazement. "Now you guys need decent haircuts and some new clothes. I will use my credit card, but no going crazy or you will pay the bill."

Threshold walked through the crowded halls. He checked out the diversity of people and the clothes that they wore. Some people were white, some brown and tan. Some people wore suits and ties, some wore jeans and t-shirts. Out of everything he had seen it seems no attire of this world expressed how he felt. He felt outcasted, hurt and alone. Those feelings drew him into a store called Hot Topic.

"Welcome to Hot Topic. Is there anything I can help you with?" asked the woman behind the counter. It was a blonde haired woman in a black tank top. She had a lip ring and a piercing in her tongue. She also had a tribal tattoo that covered her left arm.

"Right now I'm just looking," he replied. "I do think black is my new favorite color now though."

"Well if there is anything I can do just let me know," she replied with a flirty smile. "It's not every day we get Irishmen in lab coats in this place. Kinda cool." Before he could respond Buxton and Salles walked in.

"I finally found you!" Buxton exclaimed. She rummaged through her purse for her wallet. "Here, take the visa card. Indigo wants to go to another place. When you're done here meet us down at Knockouts to get trimmed up some. You really are starting to look like a caveman," she laughed. Salles and her walked out of the store.

"Oh, I see you have a lady friend," the woman said with disappointment.

"She is more like a sister. That's it," he replied. She just looked at him with a smile.

Salles and Buxton were talking as they walked into the sporting goods store.

"Tobias is so quiet and secluded. Why?" Buxton asked. Salles looked around at the clothes.

"He holds a lot of pain inside," he replied from in the fitting room. "You see, during the Demon Wars his family and all of his kind were murdered. He is the last of his kind. King Moranvale left the Jungles of Pixima unprotected from the demons. He said he tried to protect his family the best he could. Just to see them die in front of him. He was locked up in the dungeon for trying to kill the king. He escaped and I was sent to bring him back."

"If you were sent to bring him back, then why are we here now?" she questioned his response. He picked out a nice track suit to try on.

"Something about this situation just doesn't feel right to me," he stated. "Back there in the alley he mentioned the whole war was a charade. My instincts say he is telling the truth but it goes against my orders. Plus it's kinda suspicious that the bar wench followed us here." A woman in marine issued camo uniform overheard the conversation when she passed by. She forgot what she was shopping for when she heard the bizarre story. She pretended to look at the sports bras when they left the dressing room. When they left after paying for the clothes, the woman kept her distance following them.

Threshold walked out of the dressing room at Hot Topic. He was wearing a black denim jacket over a white t-shirt and matching black jeans. Finished off with tan work boots.

"Looks good on you," stated the store clerk. She started to ring up the clothes he was wearing. "It might be better after that haircut. Like your sister said. My shift ends here soon. Maybe I can meet you down at Knockouts and see how it turns out," she flirted.

"Sounds good", he replied.

"Damn. All this talking I forgot to introduce myself," she apologized. "Think I got carried away because it felt like I already know you. I'm Sandra Moyer."

"Well you do remind me of someone I once knew," Threshold replied. "I'm Tobias Threshold. I guess I will meet you down there." He smiled and walked out the store to meet the others. Heading down to the salon he walked passed a jewelry kiosk in the hall and seen a crucifix necklace he liked. Being the thief he grew to be, he reached out and took it with his cat like speed. No one even noticed it was gone. He slipped it on before finally meeting up with Buxton and Salles. He reached into his pocket to get her credit card to give to her.

"Welcome to Knockouts," said the stylist. "What can I do for you today?" Threshold and Salles both looked at the pictures on the wall to find what they like.

"I'm looking for something in a clean cut look like that," Salles replied. He pointed at the picture of a clean shaven man with short spiked hair. Threshold said nothing. Only pointed to the picture of a man with an under shave ponytail and trimmed goatee. The woman escorted them back to the barber chairs.

"Would you like any coloring today?" she asked. They turned to look at each other.

"No thanks," they replied simultaneously.

Back at Branville Castle, Alastor was explaining the process of extracting demons to Moranvale.

"You see, your majesty, the only way to get a demon out of the body is to kill the host," he explained. "To make it quick and painless you should go straight for the heart." He punched through the chest of the tall muscular man, ripping out his heart. He held the still beating heart in his hand. The body fell to the floor leaving just the dark shadow standing in its place. He then through the heart on the ground and stomped on it and turned towards Moranvale sitting in his throne. "You can kill the host in any way but beheading. Take the head, a demon will die too." He continued the process. He went down the line, ripping the heart out of the other two and stomping on them. "Someone dispose of this garbage!" he yelled. Two men came and dragged the bodies off one by one to be burned in a pit of fire. Moranvale sat back in his throne. The oracle's words ran through his head. *Beware the one who lives amongst the trees.*

"That is good to know, but what's your plan to get rid of Threshold?" he asked. Alastor strutted closer to the throne.

"That is simple," he replied. "Our master wants us to form an alliance and proceed to take over the other realm. If Threshold dies in the process that will be a plus. There are plenty of souls on the other side." Moranvale leaned forward in his throne.

"Does sound like good plan, but what's in it for me?" he asked Alastor.

"Yes that," he replied. "Well you will get to rule over both Pixima and the new world too," Alastor sneered. Lilith slammed the door open to the throne room and strutted up to Alastor enraged.

"We are going to kill Threshold and Salles for siding with him!" she demanded.

"Yes. That is the plan," he responded. That is why I let these three out of those useless bodies. He turned to face the freed demons. "You three! Go find the Marsters and use them to kill Threshold!" There was a faint whisper.

"Yes, kill the beast," they replied as they flew out the door.

The sun was setting when Butch and Ranger started to wake up Spike was awake an hour before and started the hunt for Salles and

Threshold. He followed the scent to the mall. Before going into the mall he sniffed the air.

"Demons," he whispered. He opened the door and ran through the halls. "Captain Salles! They are coming!" he yelled. He ran past Sandra who was on her way to meet up with Threshold. She started to run after Spike because she knew Salles was with Threshold. He stopped in front of the salon. "Sir, I finally found you!" he exclaimed. "Wait. You smell like the captain, but you don't look like him. What happened?" Spike was confused as he checked out Salles' new look. Salles tried to calm the boy down.

"Spike, where are your brothers at?" he asked.

"I left them sleeping in the street and came to find you. I smell Threshold nearby! We must find him before the demons come!" he panicked. Sandra finally caught up with Spike at Knockouts.

"You, you are with Tobias and his sister. Is he still here?" she asked Salles. Before he could answer she turned to Spike. "And you, weird guy, who is coming?" Threshold and Buxton walked out of the salon to show off his new look. "Now that does look good on you," she stated. She gave a little hair flip as to flirt a little. Threshold seen a dark shadow coming towards him.

"Get back!" he exclaimed pulling Sandra into the entrance of the salon. Salles sends Buxton to take cover with her. The demon flew over all the shoppers towards Threshold. He planned on taking over his body only to stop face to face with the planned victim. The crucifix that he stole was the only thing preventing him from getting possessed. The demon floated in front of his face. Threshold threw a strong straight punch that only phased through the shadow. Enraged by his failure to control Threshold, the demon tried to possess a human only to fail again. He was left with no other choice but to flee. The shadow leaves to report back to Alastor.

"Why did you bring the girl in?" Salles asked Threshold.

"Hey guys! Over here!" Spike yelled. He seen Ranger and Butch roaming around the crowd. "Captain, something is strange here. They look normal but they carry the scent of evil." The two brothers came closer to them. Salles seen their eyes were as black as the midnight sky.

"There's too many people here. We must run," commanded Salles. He went into the salon to get the girls.

"She reminds me of Estella," Threshold replied. "And I'll do what I must to protect her!" He ran down the hall towards Butch and Ranger. He started to change into his lion form while running. His new clothes ripped to shreds leaving only his tattered pants. The woman in uniform ran across the hall from her spy position.

"What the hell is going on here?" she asked Salles. "I decided to follow you after I overheard you talking."

"There is no time for explanations now," Salles answered. "Spike, you have to realize those guys aren't your brothers anymore. They want…"

"Yes, there is no time for introductions," the woman interrupted. "Ladies, come with me. You guys join your friend," she commanded.

"He is not my friend," Salles replied. She scowled at him. "Seems like there is no other option," he groaned. "Just listen to the lady. Spike come on." It took a minute for Spike to realize what was going on. He felt an emptiness inside knowing he will have to kill his brothers. Still he had to join the fight. He removed his green cloak and began his transformation. His nose and mouth conformed into a muzzle with long sharp fangs. His shoulder length brown hair now covered his whole body. He grew to an eight foot tall werewolf before letting out his warning howl. The woman helped Sandra and Buxton out from under the counter.

"It's okay ladies," she comforted them. "I need your help to ensure the safety of everyone here. My name is Lance Corporal Jeanette Hall. I'm gonna need you to be brave and rally these civilians." She pointed at Buxton, "You, take the frontside of the mall." Then she pointed at Sandra, "You, take the backside. I'll take this area and rush them to the easiest way out."

"Okay, I got this," Buxton replied. She charged towards her post. "Everyone! This way!" she yelled. Sandra stood there watching the panicked crowd afraid of what to do.

"What the hell?! I've never done this shit before!" she exclaimed.

Hall put on her cover and replied, "If you want to live just do what I say." She went off to the center of the mall. After hesitating Sandra gathered her confidence and ran to the backside of the mall.

"People! Calm down and follow me to safety!" she yelled.

Threshold had Ranger pinned down. He kicked him off and Threshold flew through a thick glass window. He slowly got up from the shattered mess.

"They are some tough sons of bitches," he told Salles.

"Yes they are," Salles replied. "But if we don't decapitate them they will just keep coming back." Butch slammed him against the wall. "That's the only way to kill a demon." he groaned. Threshold took a look at his surroundings. He picked up a long sharp piece of glass and put some distance between him and Ranger.

"Is that it!" he exclaimed. He put all his might in a lunge toward the demon wolf and jammed the glass in his throat. The gurgling sound echoed in the empty hall. Ranger choked on his own blood. Threshold planted his feet on the wall and pushed off. Still holding the broken glass. He spun around cutting through the beast's thick neck. The body changed back to human form and collapsed to the floor. Blood flowed thick out of his neck and the head rolled only a few feet away. Spike comes up behind Butch and turns him around. He felt a lump in his throat and a tear in his eye.

"I'm sorry brother," he sobbed. Spike bit down hard on the neck of his once kin. Blood spurted from the mouth of the hellhound on to Spike's fur. Before the demon could leave the body, he ripped his brother's head off. The blood sprayed to the ceiling of the mall and the body fell to the floor. He took the head out of his mouth and held it in his hand. He stared into the lifeless eyes of Butch before he dropped it by the body. Spike changed back to his human form and dropped to his knees in tears. Hall walked up and kneeled down next to him.

"I know how you feel," she consoled him. "I lost my father in battle too. It hurts but they would want you to be strong." He looked at her through his tears.

"Who are you?" he asked. She helped him back to his feet.

"I'm Lance Corporal Jeanette Hall of the United States Marine Corp," she replied. "Fresh out of basic and here on leave. You know, I wanted to see some action but I really wasn't expecting this." Threshold and Salles walked up to them.

"Thank you," Salles told her. "You were a big help back there. Hopefully no one was harmed.

"No problem," Hall replied. "We should really get out of here before the cops show up though." Without question the three men followed her towards the entrance of the mall. Sandra and Buxton were both surprised to see them in nothing but ripped up pants.

"Obviously that was a waste of money, but lesson learned," sighed Buxton. "We have been experimenting with some new fabrics back at the lab. I might be able to have the guys whip you up something to wear."

"No refunds," Sandra told her. Hall interrupted the conversation.

"Well like I told them," she stated. "We should leave before the cops come. This might be hard to explain." They all exited out the mall into the moon lit night.

BUILDING BONDS

The lone demon flew up the spiral stairs to the throne room. Moranvale was sitting in his throne talking to Alastor.

"Master Alastor," the demon interrupted. "Threshold and Salles were found."

"Good have they been dealt with?" asked Alastor. The demon hung his head in shame.

"No sir," he replied. "They got away." Alastor was furious.

"What in the bloody home do you mean they got away?!" he exclaimed.

"Now what do you mean bloody home?" Moranvale interrupted.

"It's where you're going when you die! Now shut up, old man!" he yelled.

"Yeah, that's right," he sighed. He slumped back into his throne.

"Now as I was saying," spoke Alastor. "What in the bloody home do you mean he got away! You only had one job!"

The demon began to explain, "When we arrived to take the Marsters, there was only two of the three there. I went to track down the third one and found him with Threshold and Salles. I seen the opportunity to take the lion himself, but I could not get in." His voice fizzled. "He was wearing an amulet of protection in the shape of a crucifix. Sir, I tried to take the body of a human but I could not. There will is too strong." Alastor stroked his beard in thought.

"Did you say a crucifix?" he asked.

"Yes sir," hissed the demon.

"Sounds like I have to consult with the elders," he stated. "Why didn't the others return with you?"

"They are dead. Their heads were taken," the demon replied. Alastor walked past the demon and out the door in anger. He set out on a walk down the long, dark stairwell to the oracle's chambers. He pounded on the door when he arrived.

"Open the door, you old hag!" he demanded. "I need to speak with the elders!"

"It is open!" replied the oracle. Alastor opened the door. "Come in and do as you need, but you may not like the answers you seek. For the sounds of the voices are all based on choices." He by passed the old blind woman and walked to the cauldron.

"Elders I need your knowledge. Respond to my request," he spoke. He heard a deep groaning voice come from the bubbling liquid.

"What is the knowledge you seek young demon?" asked the voice.

"The soul that we seek is protected by an amulet found in the new world. With your eternal knowledge, what can you tell me about this crucifix?" he asked.

The groaning voice replied, "The mark of the new world's savior, Jesus Christ. The son of the Divine One and protects the inhabitants of the world from our kind."

"How can we conquer this world if it is protected by this Jesus Christ?" Alastor asked.

"Influence and invitation," groaned the voice. "A ritual must be performed to cleanse the holy savior from these humans. You must first influence the right people."

"I understand," he told the voice. "I know what must be done." He went to leave the chamber. "Let me leave, hag." he demanded. She opened the door for him to go.

"I will not take your words with pique. I hope you found the answers you seek," laughed the oracle. She closed the door behind him. When he headed back up the stairs he ran into Lilith.

"I assume you spoke with the council elders?" she asked.

"Yes," he replied. They continued to go up the stairs. "They said that a cleansing ritual must take place to rid the new world of the savior."

"So I'm guessing we have to go to this new place?" she asked.

"Yes. We can't just take over anyone one there like we do in Pixima," he answered. "We have to persuade them to let us, in order to get the ritual done." They finally arrived at the entrance to the throne room. Alastor threw the door open banging it off the wall. The sound startled Moranvale causing him to jump to his feet. "We must proceed to the new world!" yelled Alastor. Moranvale had a startled and confused look."Not you. Not yet," he told Moranvale. "We have work to do." Alastor looked towards the bodiless demon. "Azazel, come with us. We are going to need you."

The three travel the night through the Jungles of Pixima. When they came to the entrance to the new realm, Lilith changed to her raven form. She picked Alastor up and flown him in to avoid the river. Azazel followed close behind. They walked the streets of Washington not knowing exactly what they are looking for. They came across an electronics store that had a television on. The eleven o'clock news was on.

"Today Senator Clint Abbott addressed Congress about a proposal for a new anti gun law," said the reporter on the television. The scene then changed to Senator Abbott's proposal that was filmed earlier in the day.

"We need to make it harder for citizens to get firearms," stated Senator Abbott. "The harder it is to buy guns the less killing will go on in the streets. It's not people killing people! It's guns killing people!" Alastor turned to Lilith with a stern look.

"Guns don't kill people. Demons kill people," he told her. Lilith rolled her eyes at him. "That's who we need to find," he stated. He walked past her to begin their search.

Buxton took everyone back to her apartment after the incident. Hall was sitting in a recliner watching the eleven o'clock news.

"What the hell?!" she yelled. "Everyone knows that undisciplined assholes with guns kill people! Just guns don't kill people! Who would believe that crap!" She points at the television from her seat.

"And in further news, last night an act of terror was committed at the Pavilion Mall which resulted in the deaths of two unidentified males," commented the reporter. "Here is what some people had to say about the incident." The picture changed to another reporter interviewing a strange old lady outside the mall. She was a short woman with scraggly white hair and a pair of thick glasses.

"Monsters did this!" she exclaimed. "I tell you it was monsters! Those men were werewolves fighting, what looked like, a lion and a tiger. I was at the pet store getting some food and catnip for my babies at home and that's when I saw them and I ran," she told the reporter. Sandra was watching from the kitchen table.

"Like anyone is gonna believe her," she commented. "Looks like she smoked some catnip herself." Salles came walking into the room. He was wearing his new track suit that Buxton had made from special material.

"Good," he replied. "We don't need anyone to know we are here. Even though we mean no one harm, who's to say they won't harm us." He glared at Threshold. "That means there is no more running headstrong into battle like that, Tobias." Buxton followed him into the room from the bedroom.

"He's right," she interrupted. "If people find out that you are from another dimension they will want to experiment on you. You don't know what goes on at the Pentagon, I do."

"Now with that being said, where is Spike?" Salles asked. Spike was out on the apartment balcony. He was wearing a pair of blue jeans and a t-shirt just staring up at the moon in the starry sky. Threshold stood up from the table and walked to the sliding glass door.

"I'll handle this," he stated. "I know what he is going through." He walked out the door to talk to him. "Hey, how you doing?" he asked. Spike still stared up at the moon.

"Good, I guess," he replied.

"I know how you feel," Threshold stated. "Those demons took my family from me too. It kind of leaves an empty feeling inside that you think will never be filled again. We have to put a stop to them before anyone else has to feel our pain." Threshold shed a single tear that fell over the railing. Spike continued to stare up at the moon.

"I said I'm good," Spike sighed. "Blood is what made us brothers. The lack of bond made us strangers. Those guys were jerks anyway, so shed two tears and down two beers. Let's do what needs to be done." Salles came out and handed them two cans.

"I'm glad the girls introduced us to this beer," he stated. "It's not like the mead back home but it does the trick." Threshold cracked open his can.

"Well if you are not out here because of your brothers then why are you staring at the moon?" Threshold inquired. Spike opened his can and took a drink to choke back his tears.

"I'm a wolf," he answered. "It's what we do." Salles patted Spike on the back and smiled as they walked back inside. Salles joined Buxton on the couch. Spike crouched down next to the chair Hall was in and Threshold joined Sandra back at the table.

"You know you remind me a lot of my wife," he told Sandra. "She just didn't have all that art work."

"Oh, are you married?" she asked.

"Was married," he replied. "I lost her and my children to those demons."

"I'm sorry to hear that," she sighed. Hall interrupted their conversation.

"You guys do know, in this day and age, soul mates don't have to be of the same race right?" she laughed. Everyone glared at her and she looked towards Spike. Blushing, she stated, "Well it's true."

Alastor, Lilith, and Azazel were still roaming the streets that night.

"Ah. This is the right place," he grinned. "I sense this is the house of Abbott." He stood under a dimly lit street light outside the two story white house. He gazed up at the top right window. "Azazel, weave me into the senator's dreams." he commanded. Azazel flew a circle around Alastor and up through the window he was looking at. Inside the room, Senator Abbott was sleeping peacefully next to his wife. Azazel stopped and hovered above him projecting the image of Alastor into his dream.

In his dream he was sitting in his congressional seat and everyone was laughing at him. It took him a minute to realize he was only wearing a pair of women's pink lace underwear. Alastor appeared in front of him wearing a white suit. Senator Abbott stood up from his seat and covered his private parts with his hands. Alastor looked at him with a raised eyebrow. He snapped his fingers and Senator Abbott was dressed in his suit.

"Senator, walk with me and talk with me," said Alastor. They walked towards the exit of the building. Senator Abbott thought they were going outside to talk but the door lead to a room. Inside the room was a queen sized bed with a canopy and red velvet sheets. In that bed was two beautiful women in black lace lingerie. One a blonde with a dark tan and the other was a Hispanic woman. Hundred dollar bills started to fall from the sky like rain. Alastor looked at Senator Abbott and asked, "Doesn't this look like a better dream?" He just nodded in response. "What if I told you I can make this a reality?"

"I would love this but I'm married and I don't want to hurt Gretchen," he responded.

"Do I look like a bad person?" Alastor asked. "I saved you from that humiliating dream. Didn't I? I'm here to help you achieve your dreams. This was just an example of what I can do. Whatever you desire can be yours."

"So you can get me anything I want?" he asked. "Sounds too good to be true. What's the catch?"

"The only catch is you have to answer yes when I ask if you will let me in," he answered.

"So I say yes, you help me get what I want and no one gets hurt?" he asked. "Are you an angel?"

"Something like that," Alastor smiled. "Now I ask you, do you let me in? The choice is yours, yes or no?" Senator Abbott took a look at the girls on the bed and the falling money. He took a minute to think. He figured it all was just a dream and none of this was real.

"Will you help me get my anti-gun bill passed and ban all guns across America?" he asked.

"It shall be done," Alastor answered.

"Then yes I let you in," he replied and shook Alastor's hand.

Outside the dream, Senator Abbott started to go into convulsions in the bed. Azazel was being absorbed into him. The convulsions were so intense that it woke up his wife.

Honey, honey! Wake up!" panicked Gretchen. She shook him until he came back up to reality. "Are you okay?" she asked. "Was it a bad dream?" He sat there in a pool of sweat.

"Yea," he replied. "I dreamt that I was at work wearing only women's undergarments." He got out of the bed and walked towards the window. "I just need to get some fresh air and I should be good." He opened the window and looked down to see Alastor and Lilith standing under the street light. His eyes turned pitch black and he smiled. Alastor looked back at him and smiled.

"Well done Azazel," he whispered. "Choices can be a bad thing." He looked at Lilith, "Now let's go back and let Moranvale know the plan is underway." Lilith transformed into her raven form and flown Alastor back to the river entrance.

"Honey, can we go back to bed now? It was just a dream," Gretchen softly spoke. She patted the bed as to invite. "If you need help going back to sleep, I can tire you out some," she smiled. The darkness faded away from his eyes. He turned around with a seductive smile and accepted his wife's invitation to join her in bed.

EPISODE 6

THE MORNING AFTER

The sun shone bright through Senator Abbott's window. The blinding light beamed onto his face. He jumped out of bed wearing only his boxer shorts just to shut the curtains fast. He usually loved the morning, but today was different. The sun hurt his eyes. Gretchen was downstairs making French toast and eggs for breakfast.

"Honey! Time to get up! You're gonna be late if you don't hurry!" he heard her yell. He stumbled from the window to the master bathroom to get a quick shower. While he was soaping up he felt he was not alone. He kept hearing a faint voice whisper his name,"Clint."

"Who's there?"He asked looking out the shower. He heard the voice again, "Clint Abbott." Wondering where the voice was coming from, he ended his shower short. He grabbed his towel and started to dry off. He walked to the sink to brush his teeth and fix his hair. He picked up his brush and looked in the mirror. The brush falls to the floor. A pair of dark eyes and a sinister smile stared back at him.

"Clint Abbott," spoke the man in the mirror. He stood there frozen in fear. "Oh you don't remember last night when you let me in?"

"Yes but that was just a dream," he stuttered. His gaze remained on the mirror.

"It seemed that way but that is how we communicate with people," his reflection answered. "Just think of me as your spirit guide. I'm here to get you everything your little heart desires. My name is Azazel." Senator Abbott calmed down a bit and collected his thoughts.

"Okay, how does this work then?" he asked.

"That's easy," he answered. "We just share this body and you go on with your life like normal. I'll just take over when I see fit." His black eyed reflection smirked at him.

"Take over?" he questioned.

"Yes. I'll just nudge you off to the side and I'll do the talking," he answered. "It's only to get you what you desire. Now you should get going before you miss out," laughed the man in the mirror. Senator Abbott snapped out of his trance when Gretchen walked into the bathroom. She leaned against the doorway.

"What's so funny, Clint?" she asked. He turned around to look at her.

"Oh nothing," he answered. "Just thinking about the fun we had last night." He gave her a kiss and walked passed her to go get dressed.

"Yea, it has been awhile for that, but you need to focus on your work right now," she reprimanded. "You are running way behind today." He looked over his shoulder after putting his pants on.

"Believe me. I am focused now," he replied. He grabbed a shirt out of the closet and put it on. "Now I just have to get my butt to work." He slipped into his suit coat and put on his sunglasses. After he grabbed his briefcase he gave her a kiss and headed out the door.

In Buxton's tiny apartment Threshold slept in the middle of the floor. He was woken by a kiss on the cheek. He rolled over expecting to see Sandra but found what he desired the most.

"Estella?" he muttered. Threshold sat up on the floor. "How can this be?" he asked himself.

"Yes, Tobias, it is true that I am gone," she answered him. "I have come to give you a message. The kids and I are in the hands of the Divine One. He sent me to tell you not to let the cleansing take place." Estella looked at Sandra sleeping on the couch. "It is alright if you care for her. I understand. She does look a lot like me. If you care for her as much as you do for me, you will heed these words and stop the demons." Her spirit floated towards the sliding glass door of the balcony.

"Estella! Wait!" he yelled. "Where is this cleansing taking place?!" She stopped right in front of the door and turned towards him.

"October thirty-first, Bohemian Grove," she stated as she faded away. He was snapped awake when Salles and Buxton walked into the room.

"I'm telling you that this can work. If we can recreate the conditions that caused the dimensional rift. We can get you guys back to Pixima where you need to be," she told Salles. He sat down at the table.

"Well it's worth a shot," he replied.

"Alright, well I have to go to work now and I will have a discussion with my team," she stated. "We can see about getting this project under way. I will see you guys later." She closes the door and heads to the elevator. Threshold sat up on the floor.

"No, we can't go back yet!" he exclaimed. He was still startled by his vision. "I know this might sound odd to you, but I just had a dream that said we aren't done here." Spike and Hall came in from the balcony.

"I think the word you're looking for is ain't," Spike said with a southern accent. "Well I'm gonna get a little shut eye now. We was up late last night."

"You sound so much like my dad," Hall laughed.

"I know. That's why I did it," he chuckled.

"I wish I could sleep with you, but I have to get back to the base," she sighed. She gave him a hug and walked towards the door. "I'll be running laps if I'm late." Spike walked into the bedroom and just flopped face down on the bed. Sandra woke up and sat upright on the couch.

"I wish I had a job to go back too," she mumbled. "You guys destroyed the mall."

"I know and I am truly sorry about that," Salles apologized. He pointed at Threshold. "It was mainly his fault. If you would just think before you react, Tobias, she would have a job to go to," he reprimanded.

"Yes. I understand that I was too headstrong at the moment, but I calmed down now," he replied. "I understand that this is not just about me anymore. I brought this upon us all."

"This is true, but I'm not a hundred percent sure I can trust your word," Salles responded. "Since we are stuck here for the moment I guess I have no choice. What is this dream of yours?" Threshold got up off the floor and joined Sandra on the couch.

"It's not the first one I had like that," he answered. "Before I found Michelle in the alley Xavier, my son, came to me. He said that the demons were coming to take over this world. He shown me things you can't even imagine. Last night Estella, my wife, came and told me that there will be a cleansing of the Divine One from this land happening."

"You see! This is why I'm not sure I can trust your word!" Salles exclaimed. "Everything you said seems a little far fetched."

"Wait. Hear him out. This might actually be something," Sandra stated. "People say the spirits of the dead can communicate through dreams. What all did she say to you?"

"She said that on October thirty-first at a place called Bohemian Grove there will be a cleansing ritual," he replied. "Well that and a few personal things I can't say yet." He glanced at Sandra. She glanced back at him and blushed.

"That does sound like something worth looking into," she replied. She pulled out her phone and started looking it up online. "There have been conspiracy theories about that place. I never believed them but they are interesting to read." Salles leaned forward in his chair.

"So you're saying that this Bohemian Grove is an actual place?" he asked.

"Yea. It's in San Francisco, California. It's a men's club used by stupid rich people, like politicians, actors and other people with a lot of money."

"What is that thing?" Threshold asked. He moved closer to her to see what she was doing.

"This?" she replied. "It's called a smartphone. It is used to call people, send messages and it holds all the knowledge in the world. Most people use it to argue with people they don't know, watch porn and look at pictures of cats."

"Cats! I hate cats!" Spike yelled from the bedroom. "Not you guys though! Just those ugly little fur balls that walk around!"

"Anyways," she shrugged. "We can look at it more tonight when Buxton gets home. We have like two months before Halloween anyways."

"What the hell is taking so long?!" Moranvale screamed at Lilith. Alastor then slammed the chamber door open.

"Don't take your impatience out on her!" he yelled. He changed his voice to a more mellow tone when he approached Lilith. "Patience my lord. Wars are won with strategy. Not foolishness."

"So what kind of strategy do you have planned?" asked Moranvale.

"You let me worry about that," he replied. "You just focus on the prize you so long for. Now you must go mingle with your people. Let them know you will be going on a long journey for awhile. Lilith will escort you and I will follow behind shortly." Lilith took his hand and walked him to the door. Moranvale went out the door first. Before Lilith left she gave Alastor a seductive smile then shut the door behind them. Alastor sat in Moranvale's throne and closed his eyes to contact Azazel.

Senator Abbott was sitting in his seat listening to a NRA lobbyist speak out against his gun control bill. The voice of the lobbyist was suddenly drowned out by the voice in his head.

"Is everything going as planned?" he heard Alastor ask.

"Yes sir, everything is good on this end," he heard Azazel reply.

"Great. Now that everything is set, let's put the plan in motion," he told him. "Now you know what to do." Senator Abbott felt like he was losing his mind. He got out of his seat and left the room. He went off to the restroom to wash his face and clear his mind.

Back in the throne room, Alastor was just waking from his meditative state. Before he could wake all the way a large black and white tiger lunged at him. He jerked himself awake falling over the arm of the throne like he was thrown. Alastor sat up into a crouch position on the floor.

"So you are still in there," he said with a smile.

Senator Abbott made his way back to his seat. He was trying to listen to what the lobbyist had to say, but it seemed he was subconsciously doodling on a sketch pad.

WANTED

"Well since there is nothing else to do until Buxton gets home. I guess I can educate you guys a little," said Sandra. "There's a special on live from congress. I think some NRA guy is speaking. Watching that might give you some idea how our government works." She turned the television to the news special. They came in after the lobbyist has said what he came to say.

"Thank you for your argument. Is there any rebuttal from the senate or house?" asked Vice President Mathews.

"Time for me to take over," Senator Abbott heard Azazel say. "I mean help you get your gun control bill passed." His eyes went pitch black and then back to normal. Azael has taken control now. He stood up from his seat and spoke. "I see you brought all the statistics on past deaths caused by guns. Bravo on doing all that research."

"Thank you sir," the lobbyist replied.

"If those are actually right though that means there are more deaths caused by knives, fists, hatchets and so on and so on," continued Azazel.

"Yes, I have covered all that," responded the man. Azazel walked down the steps towards the center floor.

"I'm sorry, I never caught your name," he stated.

"It's Willy Stanker," he replied.

"Well Willy, do you have family in town with you and how long have you been in town?" asked Azazel.

"Yes, my wife and son have been here for a few days now," Willy answered.

"Have you had a chance to take them to the Pavilion Mall?" questioned Azazel.

"No I haven't. We were gonna go today but it was closed," Willy replied. "What's this have to do with gun control?"

"Well, Mr. Stanker, let's just say that some gun violence hit a little close to home," sighed Azazel. "A mad man with an AR15 and a k-bar killed two unidentified men there a few days ago. Destroying part of the mall at the same time. "He also had a few accomplices that were unidentified also. Mr. Vice President, I seen your wife on the news. She described them as monsters. Yes this man is a monster, but a lion man? That seems a little farfetched there sir. You might want to get her checked. Think she was getting into the catnip she was buying." Everyone in the house chuckled in response. That is everyone except Vice President Mathews. He turned red in embarrassment. After the laughter stopped, Azazel stood in the center floor. He held up the sketch he did high for all to see. "This is a drawing of the suspect responsible for those deaths at the Pavilion Mall!" he exclaimed. The cameraman zoomed in on the picture of Threshold. Threshold, Salles and Sandra all looked at each other. They knew trouble was coming. Azazel stood right in front of the podium where Willy Stanker stood. "Is it true that even if we ban guns they can still be obtained illegally, Mr. Stanker?" he asked.

"Yes. They can still be obtained that way," Willy answered. "That has nothing to do with the responsible gun owners of the NRA."

"No it doesn't," Azazel answered. "But with all these regulations that we put on guns it seems psychopaths still find a way to get them. It seems to me that the only way to protect our family and friends is to confiscate all guns and let the government protect the people! This time it was two men we don't know! What about next time?! It could be your wife! It could be your child!" He looked at the camera and points. "It could be you! If we... I mean when we catch this man, who's to say there won't be another madman that will follow him? I say we destroy all guns in America and make this country safe to live in again!" Everyone was so moved by the speech that the whole building roared with clapping of hands. After a few minutes of celebration, Vice President Mathews hit his gavel on the desk to silence the congressmen.

"I'm sorry Mr. Stanker, but it looks like a decision was made," he apologized. "Senator Abbott, that was very uncharacteristic of you, but you made your point. I'll run the bill by the president tomorrow. This meeting is adjourned." Sandra turned off the television. The three sat there speechless for a minute. Threshold stood up off the couch.

"Lies, lies! All of that was lies!" he yelled. "I don't even know what an AR 15 is! Yet alone how to use one! How many people seen this?!"

"Calm down. It's just a picture box. I bet no one else seen any of it," Salles consoled.

"Not true," Sandra responded. "That was just aired in every state in America, but nobody watches that stuff. People find it to be boring. They rather watch reality shows. Believe me though. If it wasn't seen on there, it will be on the news tonight and all over the internet by tomorrow." Threshold sat back down on the couch and tried to calm himself down.

"Why just me?" he asked. "Why not you and Spike too?"

"Obviously it's the work of demonic manipulation," Salles replied. "You are seen as a threat that needs to be eliminated. You did try to kill Moranvale."

"Yes, but with a purpose," he sulked. Sandra's phone beeped with a message from Buxton.

"What was that?" Salles asked.

"Michelle just text me," she stated. "The message says, I seen the news on TV. Just lay low until I get home. We have to get you out of here. Well since we are stuck here. I guess we can see what else is on. You know, just to keep our minds off the situation here." She turned the television back on in time to catch the twelve o'clock news.

"This morning's congressional meeting erupted into an emotional debate on gun control," stated the female reporter. "Between the statistics and strong emotions brought into the room, it seems like the emotions won. Resulting in the ratification of the gun confiscation bill. If not vetoed by the president it will result in banning and confiscation of all legal and illegal firearms in the United States. This is what Senator Clint

Abbott had to say." The television changed to Senator Abbott outside the congressional building. A huge crowd behind him holding up signs.

"I have felt strongly against guns in America for a long time," he stated. "I don't care what the statistics say, gun violence is an everyday occurrence. Thanks to a friend, who wants to remain anonymous, I found a way to get my point across."

"Thank you for that statement sir. Is there anything else you would like to add?" the reporter asked. Senator Abbott blinked his eyes and they turned all black. He blinked again and they went back to normal.

"Yes there is," he answered. "This is an open invitation to all members of the Bohemian Club. There will be a Halloween party this year to raise funds for the Democratic Party for the upcoming election. Bring your wives and kids. It will be so much fun." He laughed and walked away. The television flipped back to the reporter in the newsroom.

"In my opinion, I don't think this will end well," she commented. "In other news related to the subject. The Democratic Party has announced their nominee for the upcoming presidential election. Edward Moranvale." Spike came walking out of the bedroom.

"Well this stuff keeps getting worse," he stated as he went to the fridge to grab a beer.

Alastor left the castle to catch up with Lilith and Moranvale. They were out greeting the townspeople.

"Yes, I will be leaving the area for a while," Moranvale told a young colored farm boy. "Don't know for how long. Lilith here will take my place until I return." The young man looked over at the tall beautiful woman.

"Not sure what you're leaving for, sir, but you did make a good choice on a replacement," the young man smiled. "I might just come visit the castle some time." He gave Lilith a wink. She sighed in response.

"Oh, here comes my adviser for my travels now," Moranvale stated. Alastor approached them. Passing by a group of young ladies he turned to watch them pass.

"Hello ladies, such a beautiful day to match your beautiful faces," he smiled. Then he mumbled under his breath, "Shut up you bumbling fool. I'm in control here." He replied to himself, "Are you sure about that?" He tripped himself and fell on his face. He picked himself up and brushed himself off. "Just remember, whatever you do to harm me you do to yourself. I'll live," he told himself. Lilith and Moranvale both ran to check on Alastor.

"Are you alright?" Moranvale asked.

"Yes, I just got a sudden headache that doesn't want to go away," he replied. Badgon tried to free himself from Alastor, but his soul grows weaker as time goes on. He backs down to save some strength. "Okay, I feel it clearing up for now. That's better. Now if you are done, we should prepare for our journey." As they walked away, Lilith looked back at the young farm boy and blew him a kiss. "Boy I'm going to the castle tonight," he said with a smile as he got back to work.

LIVE BROADCAST
NEWS BROADCAST   NEWS BROADCAST   NEWS BROADCAST   NEWS BROADCA

EPISODE 8

THE HUNTED

Buxton pulled up outside the apartment in a white utility van. She called Sandra's phone.

"Come to the window," she told Sandra. She went to the window and peered down at the van. Buxton was standing next to it waving up at the window. "Okay, this is what I want you to do," she told Sandra. "There is a white hooded vest in my closet. Have Tobias put it on. The others should be fine." They went to the bedroom to get the hoodie. Threshold grabbed it and put it on under his black denim jacket.

"Okay, we got it, Sandra replied.

"Good, now he should put the hood up to hide his face. Then come down here. We are going on a little trip," she stated before she hung up the phone. Sandra led the three men out of the apartment to the hall. They headed down the hall bypassing the old cat lady, Vice President Mathew's wife. She was there with one of her many cats to visit with her sister. They didn't notice her, but since that day at the mall, she could never forget them. When she made it to her sister's apartment she burst through the door to call her husband. His secretary answered the phone.

"Vice President Mathews' office. How may I help you?" She answered.

"I need to talk to my husband now!" she yelled.

"Yes Mrs. Mathews. I'll put you through right away. Would you please hold for one moment," Sharon answered. She got up from the desk, after putting her on hold, and walked to the office. "Sir, your wife is on line one. It sounds urgent." He looked up from his paperwork.

"With that woman everything sounds urgent," he sighed. "I don't have time for this. I'm about to run this bill by the president for approval." He picked up the phone, "Yes Patricia, what is it?"

"They are here!" she screamed.

"Who is there and where are you?" he responded.

"At my sister's. Those monsters from the mall," she replied. "They were living across the hall." He stood up from his desk in shock.

"Oh god, how long have they been there?" he replied.

"Dunno," she answered. She looked at her sister and asked, "Sharon, who lives in the apartment across the hall?"

She just shrugged and answered, "No one that I know. Think that place has been up for rent for awhile now."

She got back on the phone and told her husband, "She said the place is empty. No one lives there."

"Okay, I will call the FBI right now and give them the information," he said. "I'll see you tonight." He hung up the phone and looked at Sharon. "Hopefully she is right about something for once."

"What's that, sir?" asked Sharon. She locked the office door and began to unbutton her blouse. He just looked at her and smiled as he sat down at his desk.

"You know how much I would love to play around, but there is no time at the moment," he replied ignoring her advances. "I was just told that the ones responsible for the mall incident were living across from my wife's sister. I have to report this to the authorities now," he told her as he picked up the phone. Sharon buttoned her blouse up and stormed out of the room slamming the door behind her.

They finally made it down the stairs and out to the van.

"That took awhile. Why didn't you take the elevator?" asked Buxton. They started to pile into the van. Sandra was in the passenger seat and Threshold, Salles and Spike got in the back.

Before he got in, Spike looked at her and answered, "Dunno. What's an elevator?" She slammed the door shut and walked around to the driver's side to get in. Sandra decided to ask some questions after buckling her seatbelt.

"So, where did you get the van?" she asked.

"I borrowed it from work," Buxton answered.

"Okay, so where are we going?" questioned Sandra. Buxton turned the key to start the van.

"Not sure yet," she replied. "Any suggestions?"

She started to drive when Spike answered, "Considering we are new around here. You guys should decide." Salles sat there in thought.

"I'm still trying to figure this out. When and what is this Halloween?" he asked.

This time Buxton answered, "Halloween is considered the most unholy day of the year. Kids love it though. That's when they get to dress up and in scary costumes and get free candy from people's houses. It only happens on October thirty-first though. Why do you ask?"

Before he could answer, Sandra added, "Plus all these religious people out there are totally against it," she said. "They say it's the devil's night, but they offer the alternative of trunk or treat. It's basically the same thing."

"Yea that sounds creepy," Spike responded. "What do they do? Put you in a trunk if you don't take the treat? Ooooo, what if you don't like the treat?" Salles just glared at him.

"Anyways," he bypassed Spike's comment. "Tobias said he had a dream that told him there will be a cleansing of some sort on October thirty-first. When we watched the news earlier some senator said there is gonna be a Halloween party at some Bohemian Club this year. I feel they are connected."

"Well that looks like where we will be heading," Buxton replied. Her phone beeped with a text message.

It read, "Where are you? I tried to go to the apartment and the building is surrounded by cops and feds."

After reading it she said, "Right after we go back and get Hall." She stopped alongside the road and text back, "Will be there in a minute. Meet us in the alley. White van."

Agent Wallace, a tall thin African-American man, was interviewing Patricia and her sister.

"Are you sure you seen this man leaving that apartment?" he asked.

"Yes," Patricia replied. "He was with a woman and two other men. They all dressed differently."

"Well my men are searching the place and there is no sign that anyone has been in there," he objected. "No furniture or anything. Let's go men. Seems like it was a false alarm." He started to walk towards the elevator when a call came over the radio.

"Sir, there is a suspicious looking white van that has just pulled into the alleyway," said the man on the radio. Hall walked away from the crowd that surrounded the building and went into the alley. "There is a woman in marine uniform heading into the alley, sir."

"Well don't just stand there!" he exclaimed. "Follow her! Could be something important!" The agent followed Hall into the alley. She opened the sliding back door to get in only to reveal the wanted man, Threshold, to the on looking agent. He stared Threshold in the face and got on the hand radio.

"It's him, sir!" he exclaimed. "I got him in my sights!"

"Oh crap! Go, go, and go!" Hall yelled at Buxton to drive.

"All units move in on the white van! Chase them down!" Agent Wallace screamed over the handset as he ran towards the elevator. Buxton hit the gas and the tires squealed. Throwing the passengers to the back of the van.

"We have to get to the interstate!" yelled Sandra.

"No," Hall replied. "This thing is to slow to outrun them. We have to lose them in the side streets first."

Buxton answered, "She is right. We can't outrun them so we will have to lose them first."

"You should let me drive," Hall replied. "My brothers were street racers. I could lose them easy. Wish I had the old sixty-eight Camaro though."

"Not me," Sandra stated hanging on for dear life. "I like the newer cars. I would take an Audi R8. Sleeker design." Buxton smiled as she pulled a hard left around a turn. Two Crown Victorias followed close behind.

"Don't worry. I have a plan," she said speeding through a red light. Then making another sharp turn into an alley. One police cruiser tried to follow on the sharp turn only to run the other into a light pole. At the other end of the alley was Agent Wallace in his gray suit and cowboy hat. With four police cars behind him he pulled out a megaphone. The van was forced to come to a stop.

"Tobias! I know you are in there!" he yelled into the megaphone. "Just come out and turn yourself in!"

"Well that wasn't part of the plan I had," Buxton sighed.

Threshold put his hood up and replied, "Well it's time for a new plan." He slid the van door open.

"Tobias stop," Salles interrupted him. "They are only humans. Let's not do anything rash."

"Okay. Do you have a better idea?" he asked. "We are surrounded here!"

"A matter of fact I do," he grinned. A few minutes later, Agent Wallace got back on the megaphone.

"Tobias! You have to the count of ten to come out with your hands up or we will have to drag you out!" he yelled. The van door slid open and out stepped Threshold. Wearing his black denim jacket over top the hooded vest, white t-shirt and blue jeans. He had his hands in the air and his head down with his hood covering it. He stopped only a few steps away from the van.

"I will turn myself in if you let the others go!" he demanded. "They are not part of this!"

Agent Wallace turned to Patricia and asked, "Are you sure he is the one we need?"

"Yes," she replied. "That is the same outfit I seen him leave the building in."

"Alright! Just back out of the alley slowly and you're free to go!" He signaled for the officer at the other end of the alley to let them go, but follow them closely. The officer moved his vehicle out of the way for them to pass. Hall was driving now, so she disobeyed and just slammed it in reverse. She made sure to hit the cruiser so it wouldn't be able to follow. The impact to the cruiser signaled for Threshold to start his transformation, but under the hood was not Threshold. Spike dropped the hood when he started to change.

"Or maybe he was wearing different pants," Patricia stated. Spike stood before them in his giant wolf form. The clothes that ripped and torn before now stretched to form fit his body. He let out a loud howl to frighten Agent Wallace and the others. He followed the howl with a simple "Boo" before he ran off in the direction the van left. He jumped on the cars, smashing them even more.

"And everyone thought I was crazy," she said to Agent Wallace. He rolled his, turned and walked away from her.

"I want them found, now!" he cried out.

Spike ran for a little while before changing back to his human form and walking into a parking garage. Upon entering he sees three cars. A sixty-eight Camaro, an Audi R8 and a ninety-two Dodge Stealth all in black.

"Where is the van and whose are these?" he asked.

"I parked it on the third floor," Hall replied. "So if they find it will be harder to track us."

"These cars are ours," answered Buxton. Her answer only aroused Salles' suspicion.

"Where did you get them from?" Spike asked.

"Will explain later," she answered. "Let's just say they were a gift from someone upstairs."

"Oh I see," he acknowledged. "Someone you work with."

"Yea, something like that," she chuckled and patted his shoulder. "Right now we have to leave," she said as she walked towards the Stealth. "Each car has a GPS system programmed with different routes to the Bohemian Club in California. Which is on the other side of the country. We pair up and go our separate ways. That way it will be harder to find us." Threshold started to walk towards the Audi with Sandra. Buxton interrupted, "No, you are with me. We have a lot to talk about," she said. He walked back to Spike to get his jacket and hoodie back before going with Buxton.

"I hope you didn't ruin my stuff," he glared at him. He took his stuff back and went to get in the car. "I hope this stuff is washable," he told Buxton. "It smells like dog now." Spike got in the Camaro with Hall.

"He's just mad he can't ride with his girlfriend," he laughed. "At least I get to ride with my favorite partner."

"Get in, shut up and enjoy the ride," Hall smiled at him. She opened the door to get into the driver's seat.

Salles was quiet when he got in the Audi with Sandra. He suspected that something strange was going on with Buxton.

"I know this car has a lot of power," Sandra said to break the silence. "But I think I can handle it." She started the engine and revved it. The vroom sound echoed in the garage.

Hall rolled down her window and yelled, "Oh yea! Listen to this!" She started the Camaro and revved the engine with a loud rumble.

"Damn kids," Buxton muttered. The Stealth started up nice and quiet. You could barely hear the engine rev. "That's why it's called a stealth. You can't hear it coming." They all pulled out of the garage one by one and went off their separate ways.

COMING TO LIGHT

The ride was a long quiet one in the Stealth. Threshold just stared out the window as Buxton drove. The silence was broken by the sound of a little girl's voice.

"Daddy," he heard. He looked up at the rear view mirror and seen his daughter, Felicia, in the back seat. Her pale, deathly looking skin and black tired eyes stared back at him. "Daddy, not everything is as you see with your eyes," she told him.

"Yes, I know," he replied. "Demons are here in this world."

"Yes, and what you perceive as allies can be more than friends," she replied. She took off her dismembered head and sat it on her lap. Felicia waved goodbye and said, "I love you daddy. We are all okay. Trust Michelle, she will take care of you. The Divine One said so." Felicia faded out of the back seat. Buxton slammed on the brakes to avoid hitting a deer crossing the nighttime country road. Threshold was woken up after he smashed his head on the dashboard.

"See, that's why we use seatbelts," reprimanded Buxton. He rubbed his head and glared at her. She started the car again and continued to drive down the back country road. "I see you dozed off for a bit."

"I must have," he replied buckling his safety belt. "Now my daughter showed up in the back seat. These dreams are getting too intense for me."

"Oh is that right. What did Felicia have to say?" Buxton asked.

"She said that things aren't as they seem to be and some allies are more than just that," he answered. "That and the Divine One said to trust you. Hold on? How did you know my daughter's name?"

"Well that's what I wanted to talk to you about," she answered. "I'm not really a physicist at the Pentagon nor am I human. The Divine One got word of the deal of darkness and the events that follow. I was sent down as a seraph watcher to make sure you are prepared for the events to come."

"What events do you mean?" he asked.

"The almighty has chosen you to be the savior of both Earth and Pixima," she replied. "First we have to do what we can to stop the cleansing."

"What is this cleansing and how do I know this is real?" he questioned.

"I could ask the same thing about you," she responded. "You are a six foot tall lion of all things."

"Six foot five to be exact," he joked. She glared at him. Then went back to watching the road.

"Okay, I was just estimating," she scowled. "Any ways the cleansing is a demonic ritual that will banish the presents of the almighty from the lands. In return Lucifer, the supreme ruler of the Underworld, will be released to rule over everything. All life, in both realms, will be hell."

"And I'm supposed to stop all this?" he muttered.

"Yes," she responded. "You have a reliable team the Divine One assembled to assist you, including me. Just keep that crucifix around your neck and that will prevent them from entering you. It's a symbol of your faith."

"You do know I stole this, right?" questioned Threshold.

"Yea, I know. Who do you think put it there?" she answered. "I know more than you think."

"Okay, then tell me this," demanded Threshold. "If you are a seraph watcher then how do you know about all this interdimensional stuff?"

"That's an easy one," she replied. "You see Michelle Buxton is a physicist. She knows all that stuff and you know her. I didn't take this vessel until after your picture was shown on the television. My name is Gabriel. Unlike a demon I can move from vessel to vessel without them dying."

"Alright, alright," he laughed. "If you are a guy, why did you choose a woman's body?"

"Let's just say the Divine One has a strange sense of humor," she laughed.

"Okay, if you say so. Felicia did say to trust you. So we are heading to the place where you said the cleansing was taking place?" asked Threshold.

"Yes, but we have to make a stop in Denver first," she replied. "Buxton wanted to check something."

Senator Abbott was on his way to the west wing of the White House to speak with Vice President Mathews. That is until he heard Azazel's voice.

"Before you push the situation, we should talk about this," he heard him say. He headed to the men's room to avoid people thinking he is losing his mind. He went to the sink to wash his face. He looked into the mirror to see those black eyes staring back at him.

"Are you sure we can trust these people to pass your bill?" his reflection asked. "I mean look at the facts here. The president takes vacation after vacation. He doesn't care about what's going on in the world, and the vice president mainly goes to work to have sex with his assistant. The elections are coming up. Let's get a good person in office and then push it. I mean your fellow congressmen all agreed upon it, so let's just wait."

Senator Abbott heard another voice say, "Azazel, stay where you are. We will come to you."

Senator Abbott panicked and screamed, "Who is coming?!"

"Woah, woah. Settle down Clint," replied Azazel. "Don't worry. It's just the next president and his running mate." The restroom door opened and Senator Abbott swiftly turned around, nervous and scared. In walked Alastor in his black suit and red tie. He was followed by Moranvale in his blue suit and plaid tie.

"Who are you and what do you want?!" he blurted out.

His eyes went pitch black and Azazel answered, "This is the next president, Edward Moranvale, and his vice president Alastor."

"Hold on," Moranvale interrupted. "I have no idea how the system of this new world of America works. How do you know anything about it? I mean none of us are from here?" Azazel decided to answer.

"It's the perks of being what we are," he answered. "We know the knowledge of the host that lets us in. That and we have a link of communication with each other. The knowledge I get is passed on to him and so on. Now did I make that simple enough for you?" He scowled at Moranvale.

"So you mean since you both are de…" Moranvale started to say. Alastor put his hand over his mouth to shut him up.

"That doesn't matter," he interrupted. "What does matter is the knowledge I got from this body. It seems that Threshold is working with Indigo Salles and Spike Marsters," he grinned. "It's time to send our favorite pets, the Chon Chon, to track them down."

It was about four in the morning and Threshold and Buxton, or Gabriel, were driving all night. They pulled up to a twenty-four hour diner, on the outskirts of Denver, to rest and get a bite to eat. They got out of the car and noticed the parking lot was empty except for one large orange semi-truck. Inside there was a short old man with long hair and a long beard drinking coffee at the bar. Threshold sat next to the man and looked at the name tag on his grey shirt. The name tag read Ernie. Gabriel sat on the other side of Ernie and asked for a menu.

After Gabriel placed his order he asked Ernie, "What keeps you up so late, sir?"

"I'll take the meat lover's breakfast," Threshold told the waitress.

"Life is a struggle," Ernie felt compelled to answer. "I just delivered twenty thousand pounds to a retired navy captain's new house in Denver. Now I have to drive home to my small apartment and wife. I haven't seen her in about a week and a half."

"How does that make you feel knowing that you work so hard and seem to still struggle?" Gabriel asked.

"It makes me hurt inside," he replied. "I try so hard to get ahead and it seems the more I try the more I fall behind."

"I know how you feel. Life can be tough," Gabriel told him. He gently laid his hand over top of Ernie's. "As long as you have faith everything will get better." A bright light shone from the connecting hands. Ernie felt lighter and more positive.

"Waitress. Can we get this man a large coffee to go?" Threshold asked the waitress. Gabriel turned to Ernie as he grabbed his coffee.

"I know some of your kids don't talk to you a lot, but that doesn't mean they don't love you," he stated. "They just don't know how to thank you for the life you gave them. Things will get better. Don't worry. The coffee's on me."

Ernie just smiled and said, "Thank you." He walked out the door to go to his truck. He got on the phone to call his wife before he started up the truck. No one answered so he left a voicemail. "I know it's still early in the morning. I just called to say I love you and things are gonna get better. I will be home later today." He hung up the phone and started up the truck.

"What was that all about?" Threshold asked.

"I just changed that man's life," Gabriel answered. "I gave him hope and now, if he keeps his faith, everything will work out. Plus I basically just saved his life. Now for ours, that's up to us."

"Okay? What's that supposed to mean?" inquired Threshold. He then heard the shrieks and chattering of the Chon Chon that flew towards the diner. The swarm of monstrous flying heads with bat like wings and fangs screeched through the night air. "Go! Get everyone to safety!" he yelled. "I'll hold them off!" Gabriel got the waitress and cook together and hid in the walk in cooler. Right as they closed the door, they heard the shatter of glass as the Chon Chon burst through the windows. A large lion's paw reached out and grabbed a Chon Chon by the face and crushed it. Purple ooze splattered on the tables and floor. Threshold let out a roar of dominance as he swiped his claws through the air. The swarm of hundreds continued to circle around him, screeching louder and louder. They bit his arms, his neck, anything they could get their sharp fangs into. They slowly drained his life essence, yet he would not quit. He continued to fight for his life. He killed off as many as he could before his weakened body changed back to human form and collapsed to the floor. A glimmer of light shone through the shattered windows of the diner. The sun was rising, so the Chon Chon flown back to the depths of the underworld. From inside the cooler, Gabriel and the others heard the sound of silence.

"Wait here," Gabriel told them. "I'll make sure it is safe." she left the cooler and went through the kitchen. She reached the bar and looked down to see Threshold. His weakened body lying in a mess of blood, glass and goo. Gabriel jumped over the bar to see if he was still alive. "Thank the almighty," she sighed in relief. In his weakened state he rolled over to look at her.

"Yea, barely," he gasped. "What were those things?" Gabriel kneeled down next to him and put her hands on his chest.

"Lay still. This might hurt a little," she told him. The same white light she used on Ernie came from her hands. Threshold let out a long painful moan as his body lifted off the floor. She let go of him after about a minute and he crashed down to the floor.

"Damn, that hurt," he complained rubbing his neck.

"Yes, but it's better than being dead," replied Gabriel. "I just healed you. As for those things, they are called Chon Chon, flying heads of the damned. Like mosquitos, just one can be a pest and easy to kill. In a swarm they can drain your life in a matter of minutes. Speaking of, I must return to the Divine One to replenish my power. Saving you drained all my vital energy."

"Hold on!" Threshold exclaimed as he stood up. "Was the old man the reason we came here?"

"No, that was just a bonus," replied Gabriel. "You should ask Buxton. It was her idea. I just got you the cars." She turned away from him.

"Will you be back and when?" Threshold inquired.

Buxton looked around and asked, "What is this mess? Who are you talking too?"

"Long story," he replied. "Why did we come here? It's way out of the way of where we need to be?"

"I wanted to see if the rumors are true," she answered. "There might be a way for you to get back home under the Denver airport."

"Can we come out now?!" the cook yelled from the cooler. Threshold grabbed Buxton by the shoulder.

"We should go before they see this mess," he told her. They ran out the door to the car.

"What happened here anyways?" Buxton asked as she started the car.

"Like I said. It's a long story. Will tell you on the road," he answered as they sped out of the parking lot.

IN THE HEAT OF THE MOMENT

Agent Wallace was in his office looking over some files on his computer when his phone rang.

"Federal Bureau of Investigation. This is Agent Michael Wallace," he answered. Senator Abbott was on the other end.

"Agent Wallace, I have more info on the Pavilion Mall shooting case," Senator Abbott answered.

"What do you have for me, Mr. Senator?" he asked.

"Threshold is working with two accomplices," he replied. "One goes by the name of Spike Marsters and the other is Indigo Salles. I got word that one was last spotted heading towards Tennessee in a black Camaro. I will fax you sketches of the suspects."

"That's good to know, sir. Can I ask you where you are getting your info from though?" he asked.

"Let's just say that I have some people doing some research of their own," he answered then hung up the phone. He looked at Alastor and grinned.

"That should take care of Marsters," sneered Alastor. "I will take care of Salles myself."

Agent Wallace yelled to his men, "Okay, listen up! We are heading to Tennessee! Taking out the friends of the enemy brings us closer to catching the enemy! Now let's move out!"

The Camaro roared passed a farm in Crossville, Tennessee, scaring the cows. Hall had some country music playing on the radio. Spike reached over to turn the music down.

"What? You don't like my music?" Hall asked.

"Yea I do like it. I just wanted to talk to you some," Spike replied.

"Good, I've been wanting to talk to you too," she answered. "Life has been a little crazy since you guys came to town."

"Yea, just a little crazy. I'm sorry you had to get caught up in all this," he apologized.

"There's no reason to apologize," she replied. "One, none of this is your fault. Two, I've been locked up on the base and itchin' to get a little action." She glimpsed at him and back at the road. "Three, I think I like you." He raised one eyebrow and looked at her from the corner of his eye.

"What do you mean by like?" he asked. "I mean, what is there not to like? I try to get along with everybody. It's like you said things have been…"

"I don't mean like you as a friend," she interrupted. "I mean intimacy, sex, maybe even love. That word does get thrown around a lot, so I'm not sure about that. Have you ever had any of those feelings before?"

"Nope, never," he answered. "Well my brothers did pay bar wenches for sex and made me watch. Never experienced it for myself though." He blushed in shame. "I've kind of have been feeling the same way about you too." She reached over and put her hand on his thigh and gave him a smile. She turned down a dirt road that lead back to a wooded area.

"Turn around and continue onto interstate forty west," the GPS stated.

"I think we are heading in the wrong direction," Spike told her. She looked at him and smiled.

"We are just making a quick pit stop before we head on down the road," she replied. Unaware they were being followed by a black sedan, she continued to drive down the dirt road. The black sedan stopped at the turnoff to the road. The man inside picked up his radio handset.

"Sir, just spotted suspect vehicle turning down a dirt road about four miles from interstate forty," he told Agent Wallace.

"Good, do not pursue and do not engage the suspect," he responded. "Stay put and wait for backup. You don't know what they are capable of."

Hall parked the Camaro in a well secluded area. Spike was confused.

"Why are we here?" he asked. "There is nothing out here."

"That's exactly the point," she responded. She reached over and kissed him. "We can do whatever we want." She kissed him again and ran her hand up under his white t-shirt. Spike didn't know how to react. He never felt the touch of a woman before. All he knew was that her touch gave him desires only his animal instincts could handle. He began to passionately kiss her neck while unbuttoning her uniform blouse. Revealing her white lacey bra. In the heat of passion, Spike let out a loud howl that startled the approaching agents. Causing them to keep their distance.

Agent Wallace picked up his megaphone and said, "I need you to exit the vehicle with your hands in the air."

"I thought you said that there was no one here?" questioned Spike. Hall got off his lap and stared through the windshield while she buttoned her blouse back up.

"Oh man, it's that idiot again," she sighed. "I'll handle this." She stepped out of the car and started to walk towards Agent Wallace. "Sir, I don't know who you think we are, but we just came back here for a private moment!" she exclaimed.

"No mistake, ma'am," replied Agent Wallace. "I may not know your name, but I always remember a face. I know you helped the suspect, Tobias Threshold get away!" Spike goes to open the car door.

"Honey, stay in the car!" she exclaimed. "I don't need help with this one! I am Lance Corporal Jeanette Hall of the United States Marine Corps!" she began to explain. "I am on leave out here with my boyfriend trying to have an intimate moment! I have no idea who this Tobias is you are talking about! Plus if I was involved in anything illegal, that would jeopardize my military career!" Agent Wallace looked at the officer next to him and told him to run the name through the database.

"That is a compelling argument, but how do I know you are telling the truth?" he replied.

"Then you can take me in for questioning!" she answered. "I'm telling you now though, if you find out I'm telling the truth my C.O. isn't gonna like it!" she answered putting her hands up. Agent Wallace called her bluff and started to come towards her with his cuffs in hand. Spike stepped out of the car to try to help her. Before he could do anything a blinding light appeared around Agent Wallace as he continued to walk towards Hall. He stopped in front of her and turned to look at his men.

"Contact Senator Abbott and tell him I was captured by the suspect!" he told them. He put his right hand out in front of him and released another flash of light that gave them a false memory of the situation. He walked to the car and got into the back seat. Hall was confused but she walked back to the car and got in too. Both Hall and Spike turned around and looked at him.

"Who the hell are you?" questioned Hall.

"Just drive before they come around," he replied. "I'll explain on the way."

"Well then, you better buckle up," she stated. Hall slammed the Camaro in reverse to turn around and then raced off down the dirt road. Agent Wallace had to straighten himself out in the back seat.

"I'm Gabriel, the Divine One has sent me," he answered.

"Well that tells us a whole lot," sighed Spike. "One minute you are ready to take us in and the next minute you're sitting in the back seat." Hall turned on to the main road doing about ninety-five miles per hour leaving a cloud of dust behind them. Gabriel smashed his head off the window.

"I told you to buckle up!" laughed Hall. Gabriel sat back up in the seat holding his head.

"Well Spike, you will know me as a seraph watcher," he answered.

"You mean like a guardian angel?" asked Hall.

"Exactly," he replied. "My kind usually manipulate others to help those in need. Due to the severity of the situation I had to intervene myself. By the way, Jeanette, that was a good performance back there," he laughed.

"Okay, the whole time you were after us you were just protecting us?" questioned Spike.

"No, I actually took this body as a host to get you out of that situation," he replied. "There is no time to be playing around like that."

"You know what we were doing back there?!" exclaimed Hall. "What did you see?!"

"The Divine One sees everything about everyone," he answered. "Let's just say I know about the tattoo on your lower back," he chuckled. "Well my job is done here for now. You can pull over and let me out."

"But we are on the interstate," answered Hall.

"I know," he responded. She stopped on the shoulder of the highway. Before he got out he told them, "Be sure that you make it to the Bohemian Club on Halloween. Tobias needs all of you there." He stepped out the car and they took off down the highway.

"How the hell did I get here?" Agent Wallace asked himself. "What happened?" he looked down the road in time to see the taillights of the Camaro disappear down the road.

Senator Abbott walked into his house. His wife was at the kitchen table waiting for him.

"Honey, we need to talk about something," she told him. Before he could respond, his cellphone rang.

"First I have to take this call and then we can talk. Okay dear," he replied. He stepped into the next room to answer the call. "Clint Abbott's phone," he answered. Agent Wallace's partner was on the other end.

"Sir, the suspect got away and they took Wallace with them," he told him. Senator Abbott heard Azazel's voice in his head.

"What do you mean they got away?!" he yelled. Senator Abbott repeated what Azazel said.

"Wallace was walking up to arrest the girl and the next thing I know is the car and him were gone," he replied.

"Damn seraphs. I wonder which one it is?" Azazel asked himself. "Don't repeat that he told Senator Abbott.

"I don't care how you do it! Just find Wallace and the suspect ASAP!" he yelled into the phone. He hung up the phone and went back to the kitchen with his wife. "Seems like we are having a little problem with the FBI," he told her.

"I see that," she answered. "We also have a little problem." She handed him a pregnancy test. "It looks like you are going to be a father." He was shocked and dumbfounded.

He thought to himself, "How can this be? We haven't had sex in months?"

"You didn't. I did," Azazel answered. "She looked so lonely and desperate, I couldn't resist. Don't worry, it's not cheating. It was still your body, everything will be fine." Senator Abbott looked at Gretchen and smiled. He went over to the chair she was sitting in and bent down to give her a hug.

"That's great," he whispered to her.

She smacked him and yelled, "No it's not! I'm almost forty! My body isn't meant for that anymore!" He pulled her in tight as her tears streamed done her face.

"It's gonna be alright," he comforted her. "I'll be with you every step of the way."

"I wish you were a seahorse, so you know what it's like to carry a baby," she laughed through her tears.

RITE OF PASSAGE

Alastor paced back and forth in front of Senator Abbott's desk. "What do you mean they got away, Azazel?!" he yelled. "First Threshold and now, the best these humans have to offer, can't bring in Marsters!" He slammed his fist down on the desk.

"I don't know how. They seem to be getting some help of some sort," Azazel answered. "That or they are better than we thought."

"Better! I'll show them who is better! Salles is mine!" he exclaimed in anger. "The cleansing cannot be stopped!" Moranvale stood up from his seat in the corner of the room.

"Alastor!" he yelled. "Your master will never see the light of this world!" He slowly stepped closer to Alastor.

"Who are you?" he inquired. "Moranvale may not be the smartest, but he is not as stupid as to challenge me," he sneered.

"I am the seraph known as Gabriel. I was sent to be sure your leader does not succeed," he glared back at him. They stood face to face in front of the desk. "I know you will not touch me because you need this body and I the same. Just consider this a warning. End this now and there will be no consequences."

"What gives you the idea that I would just back down?" questioned Alastor. He stared into his eyes. "Only someone that fears failure would issue such a warning."

"Failure is not an option," Gabriel replied. His eyes pierced through him. "Unless it's yours." Moranvale collapsed into Alastor's arms.

"Get off me you old fool," he complained. He let Moranvale fall to the floor.

Buxton and Threshold pulled up to the airport on the outskirts of Denver.

"This is why we came this way," she told Threshold.

"Really. A big building with flying machines?" he sighed.

"It's called an airport," she replied. "Legends state that when this one was being built it was designed more like a small city. The creator didn't like the design for some reason, so instead of knocking it down they just sank it into the ground."

"Now why would they do that?" he asked.

"There are so many theories on what can be down under there," she answered. "What I'm hoping for is that there is a machine down there that can get you back home."

"I think we all would like to go back to Pixima, but not until all of this is finished," he responded.

"I know. I just want to know if I'm right or not," Buxton replied. "They say the horse protects the entrance. Can you take my camera out of the glove box? We are gonna have to take pictures of the horse while we check it out. Don't want to look too suspicious. He grabbed to camera and they got out of the car. Walking towards the sinister looking horse, Buxton started to pose for the pictures. She done her poses all around the statue looking for the secret entrance. She leaned on the tail and it moved down. The ground began to rumble and the statue slid back revealing a steep and dark set of stairs. Buxton looked at Threshold and smiled before they descended into the dark abyss. After about fifteen minutes of walking down they finally seen the light at the end of the tunnel. Reaching the bottom they gazed upon two large black buildings and a platform between them.

"Now this is exciting!" Buxton blurted out. "Looks like the rumors are true. Let's look to see if there is anything that can get you back home." They split up to search the place. Threshold got the feeling they were being watched.

"Maybe we should stick together," he said. "You never know what might be down here." Buxton was walking towards the building on the right. She stopped and threw her hands up.

"Look around you. This place is empty," she answered. "If we split up we can get out of here faster and back on the road."

Threshold said to himself, "Okay, whatever. I doubt we will find anything here anyways." He walked off towards the other building. He still felt that someone was watching his every move. In the shadows, a distance away, a strange figure looked on as he entered the building. Then it made its move.

Threshold decided to explore the building. He noticed the rooms on the first floor were set up like living quarters like it was just a giant hotel. Except there was an office in the midst of them. Inside the office he noticed a large wooden desk that had a lever locked under a glass casing. Before he could examine the rest of the room he heard a loud echoing scream from the other building. He ran as fast as he could to see if Buxton was alright. He arrived in time to see her picking herself up off the floor.

"Are you okay?" he asked while helping her up.

"I think so," she replied. "I was coming into this office and I tripped over something and hit my head on this desk."

"I was in a similar room when I heard you scream," he told her. "Did you find anything of use?"

"Actually I did," she answered. "There is a switch on the desk. If both switches are pulled at the same time on both desks a portal will open on the platform in front of the buildings." Her answer sparked questions in Threshold's mind.

He thought to himself, "I didn't tell her about the other room. How could she have known there was another switch?" He kept his thoughts to himself for now. "Now that we got that figured out, can we get back on the road now?" he asked. "We only have a matter of days before the cleansing."

"Yea, we can go now," she answered. "Can you drive? I don't think I can after hitting my head like that."

"I guess I can," he replied. "I watched you long enough to figure out how a car works." They left the building and headed towards the stairs to leave the unknown city.

Salles and Sandra drove a long stretch of desert through Arizona. Silence filled the car until Salles spoke.

"I see the way you look at him," he told Sandra.

"Who?" she answered. Pretending she doesn't know what he is talking about.

"Tobias. There is a sparkle in your eyes when you are with him," he replied. "Do you love him?"

"It's more like a like right now," she replied. "It kind of feels strange. I mean I'm a woman and he is a lion. Wouldn't that be bestiality or something?"

"I'm not exactly sure what that means,"Salles responded.

"The short answer is people that have sex with animals, but that doesn't matter at the moment," she answered. "Have you ever been in love?"

"No, but I did have a partner before all this happened," he said staring out of the window. "King Moranvale said he was injured when Tobias escaped prison. I wish I knew if he was alright."

"What's your partner's name?" Sandra asked. "Wait, you do mean work partner right?"

"Yes, what else would he be?" he befuddled. "His name is Marshall Badgon. He was, what you would say, my right hand man when it came to protecting Branville."

"Good. Since we are talking about love I thought you meant a gay partner," she laughed. "I mean I have nothing against gays or anything."

"We do have the term gay in our world. Believe me I do not like men," he grumbled. "I have been with a few women." Sandra slammed on the brakes and came to a screeching halt.

"Now don't lie to the lady Salles," laughed a voice outside the car. "You have never been with a woman a day in your life." Salles sprung out of the car. He saw his old partner wearing a suit in front of him.

"Marshall?" he questioned.

"Yes. What you see used to be the marshall. You can call me Alastor now, he sneered.

"Demon," Salles stated.

"Yes but don't worry. Your precious partner is still in here. I just can't seem to get rid of him," he laughed. "I will get rid of you though!" Alastor took off his coat and rolled up his sleeves. "Stay in the car!" Salles yelled. "I have to get you back to Tobias in one piece!"

"Yes, your precious love is next on my list," Alastor commented. He began his transformation to his true tiger form. He began to circle around Salles like he was stalking prey.

"Marshall!" Salles yelled. "I know you are still in there! If you can stop this, then do it!"

"He can't hear you," Alastor chuckled. "He is locked away for now."

"Then so be it!" he exclaimed. He took off his track suit jacket and began his transformation. His form fitted clothes held snug against his stripes. "I don't want to fight you, but I guess I have no choice!" Alastor dodged out of the way of Salles' first swipe and countered with his own claw to the face. "I see you are a little faster now, Marshall," he said wiping the blood from his cheek. Alastor just smiled and struck again. This time on the other cheek.

"He can hear you. He is just too weak to answer," Alastor replied. Salles' anger sent him into a fury. His orange and black fists flew at Alastor's face. He ducked and dodged every blow that was thrown. His body was getting tired, but his will to get his friend back was not broken.

"Marshall. I know you can hear me," he panted. "You are stronger than this." Alastor delivered a hard blow to the abdomen. Causing Salles to spew bile on the ground.

"So touching. You have to resort to hopeful words because you know you can't defeat me," Alastor laughed. "Enough playing. I'm bored of this toy. Time to finish you off!" He jumped up with both legs and landed a double kick to Salles' chest knocking him to the ground. Alastor fell on top of him. He raised his large black and white paw to deliver the deathblow. Salles stared up at the claws shining in the hot desert sun. Alastor's arm started to shake like he was holding back.

"I know I'm stronger than this. Just wanted to kick your ass for all those years of being your lackey," Badgon stammered. "Now leave. I can't hold this forever. Run, finish the mission at hand." Salles rolled out of the way in time for Alastor's fist to crash down in the desert sand. With Alastor blinded by the cloud of dirt, Salles sprinted back to the car.

"Go, go, and go!" he yelled as Sandra started the car. She peeled the tires leaving a cloud of smoke. As they drove away all they heard was a loud scream,"DAAMMNN!"

IT'S ALL A GAMBLE

Sandra drove the Audi to the border of Arizona and Nevada without looking back. They stopped at a gas station to get gas and snacks. Sandra hurriedly jumped out of the car.

"Shit is getting way too intense!" she screamed at Salles. "Who the hell was that guy?!" Salles stepped out of the car.

"That was my old partner, Marshall Badgon," he answered. "We need to contact the other and let them know what is going on." Sandra took a few deep breathes to calm herself.

"You go grab some food for the road and I'll pump the gas. When we are done I'll call Hall and Buxton," she replied. "On second thought, just wait on getting the snacks. I don't trust you to get anything good." He walked away and went into the store anyway. Sandra was more concerned with Threshold's well being. After she set up the pump she tried to call Buxton first.

"Come on, pick up damn it," she muttered after the third try. "Damn it Tobias. Nothing bad better have happened." She hung up right when the tank was full. Then she tried to call Hall.

Hall and Spike were nearing Glendale, Arizona when her phone rang.

"Yea," she answered.

"We ran into a big problem out this way," she told her. "I'm just checking to see if you guys are good."

"Just a run in with that FBI agent," Hall answered. "One minute he was gonna arrest me. The next he was getting in the Camaro talking about he was a guardian angel. That was some weird shit. Did you try to get ahold of Tobias and Buxton?"

"Yea. I got nothing," she answered. "Tried calling like three or four times. Hope nothing happened. Where are you guys at? Think it's time to meet up."

"Passing through Glendale and heading towards Nevada," she replied. "Where are you guys at?"

"Just made it to Nevada before I called you," Sandra responded.

"Okay, head on to Vegas. We can meet up there," Hall commanded. "I always wanted to go there." Sandra hung up and walked into the store. Salles was looking at a magazine waiting for her.

"Okay, let's grab a few things and it's off to Vegas," she told him. "We are meeting up with Hall and Spike there. What are you reading?" she inquired looking at the magazine in his hand.

"Not sure, but some of them look a lot like you," he answered. "They aren't wearing any clothes." She snatched the magazine out of his hands and put it back.

"Don't get any ideas," she grumbled. They walked to the counter to pay for the gas and snacks.

Threshold was speeding down the interstate not knowing what the laws of this world are. They were passing through Saint George, Utah heading towards the border to Nevada.

"Stop the car!" Buxton demanded. "Let me drive now. You are going way too fast for me."

"I told you I don't really know how to work this thing," Threshold replied stopping the car.

"My memory has come back to me now and I feel well enough to drive," she answered. She turned her head to look out the window. Her eyes changed from brown to green and lizard like. She blinked and they changed back. "You should have pulled over to the side of the road. You're lucky there is no traffic this time of day." She got out of the car and walked to the other side. Threshold slid over to the passenger seat to let her in. "So navigator, where are we heading next.

"Well this little thing says we are heading to a place called Nevada," he replied.

"Then maybe we can stop in Vegas if we have time," she chuckled and started to drive.

Hall and Spike just passed the Welcome to Las Vegas sign when Hall got a text message.

The message read, "Meet us at the garage of the Bellagio." Spike had his head out the window gawking in amazement.

"Look at all the pretty lights!" he exclaimed.

"Yep," Hall responded. "Welcome to Sin city. The one place in the world where you can do whatever you want and get away with it."

"Awesome," he chuckled. He gave her a wink and a smile. "So you think we can finish what we started back there?" he asked.

She smiled at him and replied, "Maybe later. We have to meet up with the others first." She turned into the garage and parked next to the Audi. Sandra was sitting on the hood and Salles had the door opened waiting for them.

"It's about time you showed up," commented Sandra. "Do you know what time it is?" Hall stepped out of the Camaro.

"Yea, it's like ten thirty," she answered. Spike stepped out the passenger side.

"So guys, what's going on here?" he asked.

"It seems that the demons are trying to stop us from completing our mission," Salles answered. "It might be best if we continue on together rather than separate. Has anyone been able to contact Tobias and Michelle?"

Spike replied, "Nope, but did you get to meet Gabriel yet?" Sandra jumped down from the hood of the car.

"No, but we did have a run in with an old friend of his," she scolded Salles. He stepped out of the car and slammed the door.

"That was not Badgon!" he blurted out. "That is some demon in his body! I know he is still in there!"

"Relax big guy," Spike replied. "Maybe Gabriel can help." Salles slammed his clenched fist on the roof of the Audi.

"I know nothing of this Gabriel person!" he exclaimed.

"Come on Cap, the guy claims to be a seraph watcher," replied Spike.

"What the hell is a seraph watcher?" Sandra inquired.

"It's their way of saying guardian angel," Hall answered. "He said he is gonna be around to help us out on this mission." While she was explaining about Gabriel, a small black and white cat slipped in unnoticed and crawled under the Camaro. The clouds started to roll in and thunder started to crash. All of the lights throughout the city of sin went out. Everything was dark.

"Man, all the pretty lights went out," Spike pouted.

"Shut it," whispered Salles. "Do you hear that?" The faint sounds of screeches were heard between the cracks of thunder.

"I hear something and it sounds like it's getting closer," Hall responded. "Everyone get in the cars! We have to leave now!" Hall slammed the door shut and started the engine. The cat snuck into the car before Spike got in and hid under his seat. The roar of the Camaro drowned out the incoming screeches as they sped off out of the garage, Sandra followed in the Audi. Hall looked in her rearview mirror.

"What the hell is that?!" she screamed.

"Those are the chon chon," answered a small voice. She glimpsed over at Spike.

"What? I didn't say anything," he panicked. The small cat jumped into his lap. "What the… Man I hate cats!" He threw the creature into the backseat.

"Wait!" the cat yelled. He was tossing and fumbling in the back. "Remember, I am here to help!"

"Gabriel?" questioned Hall.

"Yes," the cat answered.

"I thought you were a black guy," Spike commented.

"No, Spike, I am a seraph. I can take any host," replied Gabriel. "Anyways, those things that are chasing us right now are chon chon. They maybe small and bee like, but in a group they are deadly."

"Well, oh helpful guide, how the fuck do we handle this then?!" Hall exclaimed.

"Considering the run in Threshold and I had before, there seems to be limited options," he answered. "You can choose to fight and hope to survive or pray that the sun rises before you run out of gas." Hall looked at her gas gauge and noticed they only had a quarter of a tank.

"So you are saying there is a slim to no chance right now?!" Hall exclaimed. She made a sharp turn down a side street. "That's just fucking awesome!"

"I never said that," Gabriel responded. "This is a test of faith. The Divine One has his ways." Spike looked at her with a twinkle in his eye.

"For you I'll take my chances," he confessed. The door opened and he jumped out. He rolled across the asphalt and then leaped into the air. Changing into his wolf form, he bit down on the first chon chon that came in reach. The purple ooze squirted out the sides of his mouth. Salles seen him jump from the car.

"What the hell is that idiot doing?!" he yelled.

Buxton and Threshold were swiftly approaching the city.

"The GPS says we are coming up on Vegas but it looks so dark?" questioned Buxton. "I always heard it was the city of lights."

"Something doesn't feel right," Threshold stated. A look of fear crossed Buxton's face.

"What do you mean by that?" she asked.

"Like there is trouble ahead," he replied. "Drive faster." She stepped on the gas and sped towards Sin City. The sky was filled with a familiar sound. The obnoxious screeching of the chon chon filled the darkness along with the screams of innocent people in the streets. "Shit, the chon chon are back!" he exclaimed. "The others must be here somewhere." Buxton plowed through a crowd with no regards for human life. "What the hell are you doing?!" screamed Threshold. She did not answer. He saw Spike out there biting and swatting at the evil flying heads. He opened the door and climbed upon the roof of the Stealth. "Everyone clear the streets," he yelled. His words fell upon deaf ears. The thunder crashed and the lightning flashed. He let out the loudest roar he ever made drawing the attention of the panicked people. "Everybody find shelter and take cover!" he bellowed. The sight of a lion beast on top of a car only increased the panic in the streets. He caused most everyone to seek shelter in nearby hotels and casinos. They came closer to Spike's location as the streets cleared. He jumped from the top of the car and grabbed two chon chon in one of his massive paws and slammed them down on the street. He left a streak of purple ooze as he slid to a halt in front of Spike.

The ooze seeped out of the sides of Spikes mouth. Bloody bite marks covered his chest and arms.

"You do know how to make an entrance, Toby," he chuckled through the pain.

"Where are the others?" asked Threshold.

"Behind you!" Spike blurted out. Threshold turned in time to swat one out of the air. A wave of chon chon swarmed towards them.

"They are driving around somewhere trying to outrun these things," Spike answered. He continued to swat and chomp the flying pests. "I'm trying not to bite them but they taste so much like mutton."

"I'll take your word for it," he replied. "Why didn't you stay with them?" He shook one off his arm and threw another to the ground and stomped on it.

"Well let's just say the Camaro was low on gas and Gabriel said this was a test of faith," he answered. He bit down on another chon chon. The ooze shot out of his mouth onto Threshold's face. "See, mutton, right?" He wiped the disgusting goo from his face.

"So you got to meet Gabriel. Is he still here?" Threshold asked.

"Yea, I left him in the car with Jeanette," he answered. "If we get out of this alive, he is riding with you." Suddenly all the lights came on. They lit the whole city up like daylight. The light drove the chon chon to flee into the night sky with their horrid screeching. The sonic screams caused them both to drop to their knees and cover their ears. Once the air cleared they both looked up at each other. Threshold glared at Spike with a stern look.

"Don't ever call me Toby again," he scolded him. He stood up and walked towards the Audi that just sped around the corner. Sandra got out of the car in a hurry.

"Where the hell have you been?! I've been trying to call Buxton and I get no answer?!" she complained. The tension was high with their faces only inches apart.

"I don't know. She must have lost here phone," he consoled her. She caressed him in her embrace.

"I've been worried about you," she told him. Ending the embrace she asked, "Where did she lose it at?"

"We were investigating a place Michelle said might be able to get us back home," he responded. Hall walked up behind the car with the little cat following behind her. Gabriel walked up to Spike and nuzzled his leg. His wounds began to heal. "We can talk more about that later. What's going on with that cat though?" he asked. Gabriel jumped up into Spike's arms and the rest of his body begins to regenerate.

"You might be useful to keep you around after all," Spike said as he fainted on the ground.

"That's Gabriel. I believe you met before,"Hall answered. Gabriel started to approach Threshold.

"No, I'm ok for now," he stammered backing away from him.

"Let's not forget about the mission at hand," commanded Salles. He walked over to Spike lying on the ground. "Help me get him in the car so we can get their car moving." Threshold helped carry Spike to the Stealth. They struggled to get him in the back of the two door car.

"Damn that's a tight fit," Threshold stated as they finally got him in the seat. Hall climbed in next to Spike.

"Can we just go get some gas for my car now?" she demanded. Buxton started to follow Sandra to the gas station when Gabriel came out from under the seat. He curled up in Threshold's lap and began to purr.

"I could get used to this body," he stated. Threshold slowly drifted off to sleep as his wounds began to heal.

A SLITHERING MISTAKE

Senator Abbott burst through the door of his comfortable home. His eyes pitch black.

"God damn chon chon!" he screamed. "They are useless!" Gretchen was in the kitchen stirring pasta for dinner.

"You keep talking like that and you're going to hell when you die," she scolded him. While dicing onions for the sauce, she accidentally cut her thumb.

"I think I already know that," he replied. He walked into the kitchen and set his briefcase on the floor. "Dear, may I ask why you are sucking your thumb?" he inquired. She dropped her hand to her side. The blood gushed from her thumb and dripped upon the floor.

"I heard of strange cravings when you're pregnant," she sobbed. "Things like pickles and peanut butter, but I never thought blood would be on that list. Is there something wrong with me?" Senator Abbott embraced his wife.

"No, no. There is nothing wrong at all," he comforted her.

"Good, good," Azazel laughed in his head. He brushed off those words and went back to his sobbing wife.

"Maybe spaghetti is a bad idea for tonight," he suggested." Maybe we can go out for steak instead and save that for tomorrow night." Azazel had another idea. He pushed Senator Abbott off to the shadows.

"Or I know the person to see about those cravings," Azazel chuckled. Gretchen pulled out of her husband's embrace.

"What are you suggesting, dear?" she asked. He looked at her with a smile.

"You have to give the baby what it wants, right," he answered. "I just happen to have a friend that can help with that. Trust me." Gretchen was confused.

"What about the dinner I prepared?" she asked. "That and I'm bleeding all over."

"I can help you bandage that up," he answered. "After we put the food away I can give him a call and let him know what is going on." Little did she know, Alastor already knew they were coming, due to the link between demons?

"Okay, if you think it will be alright," she sighed. He walked to the cabinet to retrieve the bandages.

"Everything is gonna be fine!" he yelled from the bathroom. "Have I ever lied to you?!" He sneered while closing the medicine cabinet. His reflection in the mirror muttered, "What is going on? Is my wife okay?" Azazel just smiled and walked away.

Senator Abbott and Gretchen pulled in front of a white Victorian house with a crimson red door. Alastor had already prepared the meal for the night. It consisted of raw calf liver as an appetizer. Followed by a steak so rare it will satisfy her bloodlust. Topped off with the freshest of caviar. Alastor put on his gentlest persona when he heard the doorbell ring. He answered the door with his white shirt unbuttoned and his hairy chest peeking out.

"Please excuse my appearance. I have had a long day," he claimed. He started buttoning his shirt. "Do come in." They both followed him inside.

"I really love your home," Gretchen stated. They walked towards the kitchen.

"It is what it is," Alastor replied. "The dining room is this way." He sat at the table and stared at Gretchen. "Your husband tells me you have a strange craving for blood, now that you are with child. How long have you had that?" he inquired.

"I don't want to sound odd or anything," she sighed. "It only started today when…"

"You accidentally cut yourself," Alastor interrupted. "It's not odd at all. Developing children need the extra nutrients from the blood to reach full development faster. That is the way of evolution. You have come to the right place." Gretchen looked at the food upon the table. The sight of the liver makes her stomach turn and mouth water at the same time. "Well you can have a seat and enjoy as much as you desire. I have a business matter to discuss with your husband." Alastor and Azazel left the room to the den down the hall. Residing comfortably in the leather chairs in front of the fireplace, they began to discuss the matter at hand.

"First off, how did you get such a nice house?" asked Azazel.

"Never mind that," demanded Alastor. "We have to address the matter at hand. We have to put an end to Threshold or our plans to rule both realms will be ruined."

"So that's why you left Lilith have the throne?" Azazel inquired.

"Yes, she can watch over Pixima while we watch over this America," he answered. "The cleansing is to have our father replace the Divine One as ruler over both lands." Azazel sat back in deep thought.

"I think I have an answer!" he blurted out.

"Quiet you fool," hushed Alastor. "You forget the senator's wife is down the hall?"

"Oh yea. Well since the chon chon didn't work out, why not use the serpent?" he whispered. A smile came across Alastor's face as he stroked his beard.

"Yes," he replied. "Have the senator go check on the misses and I will work a deal with Indombe." Senator Abbott stood up from his seat and went to the kitchen.

"How are you doing, honey?" he asked. She turned to him and smiled. The blood from the liver drenched her face. "I think you need to clean up before we go home."

The traffic was easy flowing through the Sierra Mountains of Southern California. The leaves of the trees were dancing in the wind. Sandra and Salles lead the pack on their way to Bohemian Grove. Salles sat back pondering. *Why are we leading the way? It's like Buxton forgot all about the mission,* he thought to himself. He was woken up from his reflections when Sandra brought the car to a halt. Spike jumped out of the Camaro.

"What the hell are we stopping for?!" he screamed. It seemed a tree has fallen in the middle of the road. "Oh, it's just a tree. Let's just move it out of the way." He morphed to his werewolf form and approached the fallen tree.

"No! Spike stop!" Gabriel exclaimed. The small cat jumped from the car. "That's not a tree! That's Indombe!" Spike did not hear the warning. Hall stepped out of the car.

"What's Indombe?" she asked. Gabriel jumped up on the hood of the vehicle.

"Indombe is life itself but a slave to death," he replied. "A serpent to dwarf all serpents." Spike used all his strength to lift up, what he thought was, the heavy tree. Threshold and Salles both got out of the other cars with a bad feeling.

"Hey guys! It's not that heavy!" he yelled. "We should be back on the road in no…" His words were cut short when he was whisked away on the serpent's back. "A little help here!" he screamed. The head of Indombe towered over the massive trees.

"Ladies! Get these cars and yourselves to a safe place!" commanded Salles. "We won't be able to make the destination if we don't have them!" The gargantuan snake swooped its head down in front of Threshold and Salles. The hot breath blew their hair and clothes rustling in the stench.

"Threshold," hissed Indombe. It flicked its tongue to taste the air. "You shall not go any farther."

"On what grounds?!" questioned Threshold.

"The demons shall rule this world and you can't stop them," she replied. Spike finally got off Indombe's back and stood with his comrades. He let out a loud howl and charged at the serpent. Threshold looked towards Salles.

"There is no time to think. We need to act," he stated. His rage fueled his transformation. The lion let out a heart stopping roar before he joined Spike in the battle.

"He is right," commented Gabriel. "You need to defeat it before nightfall. That's when she gains her true power."

"Any ideas?" Salles asked sarcastically. "It's an enormous snake that stretches for miles!"

"Indombe is an African legend. A warrior by the name Itonde defeated her. He cut the head off and ate everything but the head that he kept as a trophy," he replied. "Most of it is merely a ghost. Destroy the head and the rest shall vanish." Salles contemplated the words he was just told. He watched Threshold as he bit and clawed at the heart of the goliath beast. Fire spewed from the chest of the monster. Threshold swung onto Indombe's back in time to get out of the way. The flames sparked a fire in the surrounding trees. An idea sparked in Salles' brain as he watched the enormous tree burn. Indombe lunged and snapped at him. He dodged out of the way and transformed into his tiger form. He charged at the beast and jumped up on its back. He worked his way over to where Threshold was riding and looked back to see Spike running full speed down the spine of the serpent. He jumped over both of them and landed on Indombe's head and dug his claws in. His attack barely made a dent in the skull and Indombe laughed.

"How do you expect to defeat me?" she hissed. "I am fire, I am mother! I am life, I am death!" Threshold's vengeful rage drove him to jump on the face of the monster.

"You are nothing!" he yelled as he clawed his right eye.

"Yes, Tobias!" Salles screamed. "Take out her other eye, too!" He jumped off her back and dashed off towards the burning tree. Threshold roared in the face of the behemoth and clawed her other eye blinding her completely. Spike was curious of what Salles was up to, so he followed him to the wooded area. He ran up the serpent's head and jumped off. The force slammed Indombe's head upon the asphalt beneath them. Threshold flew off the face of the massive monster in time to notice the burning tree crashing towards them. He dove out of the way as the log crashed down upon the beast's head crushing it.

"Eat all of me or I'll forever haunt you as a ghost," Indombe hissed her last breath. The body of the beast vanished leaving only the crushed head under the burning log.

"Think I'll pass," chuckled Spike. He looked towards Threshold. "You hungry, Toby?" they both scowled at Spike.

"Just move the damn tree. Tobias, go tell the girls the road is clear," commanded Salles. Spike lifted the burning tree off the crushed head and rolled it down the mountain. He then kicked the head down after it.

"Was the log still burning?" questioned Salles. Spike peered down the mountain.

"I think it went out!" he exclaimed. Sandra and Threshold pulled up followed by Hall and Buxton bringing up the rear. Hall rolled down the window of the Camaro.

"You boys done yet?!" she exclaimed. "Let's get going! We have deadlines here!"

"Looks like you are riding with Michelle now," Spike told Salles as he went to get in with Hall. Salles past by the Audi when Threshold stopped him.

"Keep an eye on her. She has been acting strange lately," he told him.

Before Salles got in the Stealth Buxton mumbled to herself, "You shall be avenged my goddess." She smiled when Salles got in. "Is everything good to go now?" she asked.

"We cleared the path," he replied. "We should be good to reach the destination soon."

"Great," she replied. Her smile turned into anger. "Those demons will suffer." Everyone revved their engines to signal that they are ready to race off into the sunset. Smoke from the burning tree rose towards the road as they drove away from the scene.

THE HEAT OF THE BEACH

The time was drawing near. There was only five days until Halloween. Alastor and Azazel were having Moranvale fitted for a fresh new suit for the occasion.

"I need you to spread your legs sir," stated the tailor. He ran the tape up Moranvale's leg.

"Is all this necessary," Moranvale asked. "Why can't I wear my traditional garments?"

"Because no one will take you serious dressed like that," answered Alastor. "This is a whole new culture. It's necessary to look the part. You do want what the oracle said to be true, don't you?" The tailor finished with Moranvale's measurements.

"We are done for now," he said. "Your new suit will be finished by tomorrow." Moranvale stepped down from the platform.

"Yes I do, but has the problem been taken care of?" he asked.

"I think it has been taken care of," Azazel answered. There was a television in the corner of the waiting area. A news flash came on as they headed to the exit. They stopped to watch before leaving.

"Breaking news," the reporter stated. "An uncontrollable forest fire burns in the Sierra Mountains in California. Right now the cause is unknown." When they walked out the door, Alastor put his hand on Moranvale's shoulder.

"Looks like it was all taken care of," he chuckled.

The crew stopped at a small gas station on the outskirts of Santa Barbara, California to fuel up. Hall was pumping gas when they heard the news flash come on the radio. Threshold was sitting on the hood of the Audi when Spike came out of the store.

"I thought you said the fire was out, dumbass!" he yelled at Spike.

"Well I didn't see any smoke or fire when I looked," he mumbled chewing on his beef jerky. Sandra followed him out carrying some groceries.

"There's nothing we can do about it now," she claimed. She leaned up against the car next to Threshold and stared into his eyes. "The only thing we can do now is continue on and hope the fire company can handle it." Threshold slid off the hood.

"Yea, you're right," he sighed. "Can't help but to think that it would have been prevented if… someone would think before he acted!" Buxton pulled up to the pump next. Salles stepped out of the car.

"Look at yourself when you say that!" he scolded Threshold. "I think this whole thing would be prevented if you done the same!" The tension was rising as they stood face to face. Threshold shoved Salles away from him. Hall ran between them to prevent a fight from breaking out.

"Wait!" she yelled. "I know things are stressful at the moment. That's what war is, stress. We have a few days before deadline, so why not take some time to relax and strategize."

"Yea, the beach isn't too far away from here," joined Sandra. "We can take a time out there. Take a swim. Make some plans."

"I'll go but I'm not swimming!" Buxton yelled from the pump. "I don't have a swimsuit!"

"Who said anything about swimsuits?" Hall answered with a smile. "We are looking to lose a little stress right?"

"I'm not swimming," Buxton objected. She got back in the car and noticed in the distance the black cars coming up the road.

"If we are all in agreeance, let's make it a race!" Sandra blurted out. "First one to the beach wins!"

"What's the prize?" asked Spike before he got in the Camaro.

"We will figure that out when we get there," Sandra replied. Salles and Threshold scowled at each other as they walked back to their rides. A few minutes after they raced away, Agent Wallace pulled in with two other cars behind him. The tall slender black man stepped out of his car in his cowboy hat and black suit.

"You fill up and I'll see if this guy has any info," he told his partner. He got out of the car and headed into the store. A bell rang when he opened the door. A short chubby man with balding brown hair was at the counter. Agent Wallace pulled out his picture of Threshold and showed the man. "Have you seen this man pass through here?" he questioned the man. "Most likely traveling in a pack. Three men and three women." The man squinted to see the picture.

"I actually have," the attendant answered. "A group matching that description left a few minutes ago."

"Great, do you know where they were heading?" he asked. The attendant scratched his head in thought.

"I did step out for a smoke before they took off," he replied. "Seemed like good kids. Said something about racing to the beach. Oh yea, they mentioned something about that forest fire too. The one in the picture here called another one a dumbass for not making sure it was out." Agent Wallace put the money on the counter for the gas.

"Thank you for your time, sir," he told the man. He walked away and mumbled to himself, "That's another charge on them." He threw the door open and the bell rang loudly. "Let's move out!" he yelled. "They're heading to the beach near here!" They all scrambled to their cars. Agent Wallace got in the driver's seat and looked at his partner. "We gonna get them boys this time, Cletus," he laughed. His partner glared at him.

"Sir, I'm not Cletus," he replied. He sped out of the parking lot.

"Like you never watched that show," he mumbled to his partner.

The sun was setting and a fire was burning on the beach sands. Hall and Spike cuddled up next to the fire while Threshold and Salles discussed a strategy.

"All I'm saying is it would be easier if we knew the territory before we just walk up to the front door," stated Salles.

"And all I'm saying is, I don't see why we just don't walk in there and start taking some demon heads!" Threshold replied. The argument went back and forth. Sandra noticed Buxton standing by the water's edge staring up at the moon. She got up and walked towards her. She has been wondering why she has been acting so strange lately.

She stood by her side and asked, "Beautiful isn't it?" Buxton stood there in silence. Sandra let out a big sigh. "Are you worried about this cleansing thing?" she asked. She felt something furry rub her leg.

"I am a little bit," commented Gabriel. Right before he jumped into her arms.

"It's not that," she answered. A tear rolled down her cheek. "You wouldn't understand." Hall ran past them.

"How about a swim?!" she yelled to Spike.

"We don't have any swimsuits," Sandra answered.

Hall grinned and replied, "Who said anything about swimsuits?" She unbuttoned her blouse and threw it into the sand. Followed by her pants and undergarments. When she was completely nude she dove into a crashing wave. Her black hair shimmered in the moonlight when she popped up from the water. The light reflected off the water to show off her bikini tanned perky breasts. Sandra felt a breeze blow right past her and a big splash that followed. She looked around to see what it was. She noticed a trail of Spike's clothes leading to the water. He dove under a wave and popped up in front of Hall.

"This is strange," she said to Spike. "It's the middle of fall and the water is still warm." Buxton was talking to Sandra back on the beach.

"I'm just worried about my people," she tried to explain. "We are a strong race, but what if the demons wipe us out too?" There was a moment of silence between the two. The silence was interrupted by the sound of Hall's phone ringing in her blouse pocket. Before Sandra could check it, she notice flashing lights in the parking lot.

"It looks like we can add indecent exposure to the list of charges now!" screamed a loud voice. Agent Wallace and his men caught up with them.

"That's a matter of opinion!" Spike yelled back. "I think she has a very decent exposure!" he laughed. Hall blushed and smacked him in the back of the head. Agent Wallace descended the sandy slope that lead to the beach. Threshold stepped towards him. Salles stuck his arm out to hold him back.

"What are the charges against us?" asked Salles.

"It's not you that I was told to bring in. All I want is him," he answered.

"That was not the question. What are the charges?" Salles demanded. "You followed us all over the country. For what reason?" Agent Wallace put his hands up and backed away.

"I've seen what you are," he claimed. "Well at least him." He pointed towards Spike.

"Put some damn pants on!" Threshold yelled at him.

"The last thing I want to do is make you mad," Agent Wallace complied. "My orders are to bring in Tobias on the charges of murder at the Pavilion Mall. Also witnesses placed you in the Sierra Mountains before the fire started. I'll let the indecent exposure slide this time."

None of that was my fault!" exclaimed Threshold. We were attacked by demons! We were defending ourselves!"

"Okay, then how did the fire start?" asked Agent Wallace. Before anyone could respond a huge splash was heard by all. They looked to see what it was. In the light of the moon was the gargantuan serpent, Indombe.

"You were warned," she hissed. "Eat all of me or I'll be back." She blasted a flame towards Spike as he rolled out of the way. The fire was hot enough to change the sand to glass. Hall fled the water and grabbed her clothes before retreating to the parking lot. Sandra took Buxton's hand and followed her. Hall's phone flew out of her blouse pocket as they fled to safety. Threshold pointed at Indombe.

"It was her! She started the fire!" he yelled. Agent Wallace stood there dumbfounded, mouth wide open. His men fled back to the safety of their vehicles. Threshold began his transformation when he was suddenly stopped by Salles.

"Stand down!" he commanded.

"I don't think I can hold out!" Spike replied. He dodged another fire blast from Indombe.

"You are not the boss of me," Threshold said with anger.

"I said stand down!" Salles scolded them. He stared down Agent Wallace. "If we save your ass will you let us go?!" He did not answer. "If we protect you will you help us?!" he exclaimed. Agent Wallace stared at the massive monster with fear in his eyes.

"Yes, yes! I'll do anything!" he screamed in fear. Salles changed form and stared down upon him.

"Good. If you don't comply you will be next! Now run!" he told him. "Now!" he yelled. The other two knew what he meant and began their transformations. Salles ran down the beach as fast as he could. "Remember, we must eat the head in order to defeat it!" he exclaimed.

"That just sounds nasty!" replied Spike as he leapt into the sky.

"Just think about the girls and do it for them!" responded Threshold. He rolled out of the way of another flame. Spike landed on Indombe's head and stared out at Hall putting her blouse on. Then he took his first bite. The bone of the skull cracked under the tight grip of his jaws. The beast felt the extreme pain and lunged at Threshold. He jumped out of the way and landed on the other side of Spike.

"This is for you, Sandra," he muttered to himself. He took his first bite crunching into the skull. Blood and brain fluid oozed down the side of the serpent's head. He let out a roar of dominance over the snake. Salles came around the backside through the water. He sprinted up Indombe's back.

"This is for Pixima!" he screamed. Agent Wallace was frozen in fear as he watched the events unfold in front of his eyes. The idea of werebeasts battling a giant snake was inconceivable, until he seen it for himself. He heard every crunch of the bone. He saw every drop of blood and ooze spill from Indombe's head. All of it made his stomach turn. The enormous serpent finally gave up the struggle and crashed onto the sandy beach. Her body made a giant splash in the ocean.

She muttered her last words, "Eat all of me or I will…" The threat was cut short when Spike scooped out the last chunk of brain.

"Yea, yea. We get it," he mocked her chomping it down. After they swallowed down the last bits of bone and flesh, Threshold and Salles both roared together. Spike followed with a howl of triumph over the monster. Agent Wallace seen the three running towards him. Changing back to their human forms as they approached.

Salles stopped in front of him and said, "Now will you…" His words were interrupted when Agent Wallace puked on Threshold's boots. He tried to retaliate but again Salles held him back.

"I don't understand why he is puking. It's not like he had to eat it," Spike laughed.

"Now that we are done with that. You agreed to help us, or else," threatened Salles. Agent Wallace stood up and wiped the mess from his mouth.

"Sorry about that,' he apologized to Threshold. "After seeing that I have no choice but to believe you. Follow me back to the car and please will someone explain what is going on here?!" The three of them followed him up the sand dune towards the parking lot. On their way back they began telling him their tale. Who they are and where they are from. Also about the demons that want them dead. The conversation was interrupted when they reached the parking lot.

"I must have dropped my phone," Hall complained. She searched her pockets and in the car. "Did you guys see my phone when you were down there?" she asked.

Spike answered, "No but I will help you look." they ran down the dune together.

"So you are telling me that the senator is a demon and is trying to have you killed?" questioned Agent Wallace. He opened the car door to get in. "I knew politicians were assholes. Never seen that coming though." He got on his computer in his car and looked up a map of the Bohemian Club. "It's not much, but it's a blueprint of the place. If I can assist you guys in anyway just give me a call." He wrote his number at the bottom of the print out and gave it to Salles.

"Thank you," Salles replied. He folded the map and put it in his pocket.

"I found it!" Hall yelled from the beach. She picked up her phone and checked to see if it was working. When the screen lit up she noticed there was a missed call. She checked to see who it was and her face turned ghostly pale. Spike ran over from where he was looking.

"What's wrong?" he asked. "You don't look so good." She showed him the phone. The top of the call log read, missed call, 10:46 pm, Michelle B. Hall checked the voice message she left.

The message said, "I've been looking for a signal for days now. Tobias left me in this underground station under the Denver airport. My phone is about to die, hopefully I don't. If you get this message please help me. Tobias knows where it is. End of message. They both stared up at the parking lot.

"Well if that's not Buxton then who is it?" questioned Spike.

"I'm not sure but we really don't have time to go back," Hall replied. "Let's just act like we know nothing and see how this plays out." They headed back to the lot. Salles and Threshold were finishing up talking to Agent Wallace when they got there.

"Remember, if you need me call me," commented Agent Wallace. He and his crew backed out to leave.

"Yea, we should leave here too," Threshold stated. "It's only a matter of time before people come to see what happened here." They all walked back to their vehicles. Hall stopped Salles before he could get in the Dodge with Buxton.

"Keep a close eye on her," she whispered. "She may look like her, but she isn't her. Will explain later." He got in the car while Hall walked back to the Camaro.

"What was that about?" Buxton asked.

"Oh nothing important. She just needs to find a restroom," he replied.

PROPER PREPARATIONS

Buxton was locked up underground for a couple of days. She has not given up hope. Unable to contact anyone on the outside, she began to think.

"Well the phone is dead now, "she told herself. "I got to think so I don't end up the same way. An average human can survive three weeks without food and one week without water. But I'm hungry now," she whined. "If this was a game there would be a sandwich in a chest around here somewhere." She stood up off the steps and decided to search the buildings. "There has to be a kitchen or something in one of these buildings," she muttered to herself. She went into the tall building on the right and started to explore. Questions began to swirl in her mind. *Why would Tobias leave me here? Was he worried about my safety? How did he leave? He can't drive.* She rummaged through the desk drawers in the office Threshold found. She came across some documents in a folder and began to look them over.

THE D.I.A. EXPERIMENT

The Denver International Airport was built to house an experimental science program.

Funding: The New World Order.

Project Description: Manipulation of protons and electrons in extreme heat and cold conditions using strong magnetic force in hopes to open a black hole.

RESULTS

After weeks of testing the project was a success. Using an amplified amount of Gauss (magnetic flux density) the rift opened. Dr. Martin Cosgrove was the first to enter the portal. He discovered a land filled with humanoid beings with the ability to morph into creatures. Dr. Cosgrove fled back through the portal after witnessing a battle between the creatures. He requested that the project be terminated. Upon his request he vanished. Never to be heard of again.

CONCLUSION
D.I.A. Project: terminated

Buxton flipped through the other pages in the folder until she came across a diagram showing how it works.

"Boys! You are going home!" she exclaimed. She slammed the folder shut and placed it on top the desk. "That is if they come back for me," she sighed. She shuffled slowly out the office to continue her quest for food and water.

Alastor and his lackeys were setting up for the upcoming Halloween festivities. Alastor stood and watched as Azazel commanded the others.

"You! Over there! I said the stones have to be straight!" Azazel screamed. "This is a fundraiser! Not a freaking' kids party!" He ran down the steps of the stage. Moranvale approached Alastor and gazed upon the men working.

"What is all this about anyway?" he asked. Alastor looked at him and back at the workers.

"You see, stuff here doesn't work the same way it does in Pixima," he answered. "All the people that show up tomorrow determine who will be president of this land called America. The wealthy and the powerful.

We keep them entertained and they will get you what you want." He continued to gaze upon the grove. Azazel walked back up the steps.

"The pentagram has been placed perfectly now," he snickered. "The main attraction is now ready for tomorrow night."

"Good," Alastor replied. "With Threshold and his crew out of the picture, everything should go as planned." Moranvale looked confused.

"What do you mean by that?" he asked. Alastor and Azazel just walked away.

"Alright everyone!" Azazel yelled. "You all have done a great job! Now let's clean up and go home! Except the guards, make sure no one enters until tomorrow night!" Moranvale shrugged off the lack of response. He fantasized about his upcoming presidency as he followed Alastor back home.

Salles sat in silence contemplating the facts of the situation. He looked over the blueprints to strategize a plan of attack but he was distracted by another problem. Who was he really riding with? He knew she hasn't been acting herself lately, but his curiosity peaked after Hall mentioned the phone call. Due to the lack of time left he knew not to press the subject.

"We should regroup with the others to strategize a plan," he told Buxton.

"How will we do that?" she asked.

"Well if you didn't lose your phone we could have messaged someone!" he scolded her. "I guess we can move up to the front of the pack and lead them somewhere." Her face turned bright red and she stepped on the gas. They sped passed the others and Salles signalled them to get off at the next exit. He spotted a small burger joint when they got off the exit ramp. "Pull in here," he told her. "We can get some food and discuss." They pulled into the parking lot one after the other. Threshold got out of the car and did not hesitate to confront the imposter.

"Tobias! Stop!" Sandra screamed. He marched with a purpose towards Buxton. He slammed her up against the car.

"You made a fool of me!" he yelled. "Who the hell are you?!" The shock from smashing on the car made her eyes change. Threshold stepped back in disgust. "I should have known. You're a damn cold blood." Sandra was confused and scared.

"What's a cold blood?" she stuttered. Before he could answer Buxton confessed.

"I am Lesa Elza. A reptilian from the forgotten deserts of Pixima," she claimed. She changed from her Buxton form to her green scaley form.

"Oh god! Change back before someone sees you!" Hall exclaimed. Lesa looked around at the surrounding area. She seen a little boy, about six years old, looking out the restaurant window. She morphed back into Buxton before anyone else noticed. "Thank you. A lot better," Hall sighed in relief.

"Let her go Tobias!" commanded Salles. Threshold let her go and backed away. "Considering the facts here, I'm not sure if you are trustworthy. We really don't have time for this though, so I only have one question for you." Lesa looked at him confused. "How do feel about demons?" Her eyes changed from confusion to pure anger and hatred. She flicked her long pointed tongue out to sniff out demons.

"I can't stand them!" she exclaimed. "I escaped to this place to flee from the Demon Wars. I was stuck in that dungeon left to scavenge for insects in the tunnels to survive." Lesa was ready for a fight now.

"That is all I need to know," sighed Salles. He turned and walk towards the restaurant. Everyone stared at him distraught about what just happened. Salles stopped and looked back at Lesa. "I apologize for eating your goddess. It was a sacrifice for the greater good." Spike put his hands over his eyes.

"Why did he have to bring that up? I just got the taste out of my mouth," he sighed. They felt he was right, so they followed him to the door. Threshold was nice enough to hold the door for a couple and their son to leave. The little boy stared at them as he walked behind his parents.

"Don't worry kid," he told the boy. "We are the good guys." He looked at Threshold and smiled before he ran to catch up with his parents. They seated themselves at a corner booth big enough to seat them all. Salles pulled out the blueprint of the club.

"So what's the game plan?" he asked.

EPISODE 16

THE END IS NIGH

It was the morning of Halloween and the sky was partly cloudy, the sun shone bright enough through the window to wake Moranvale from his slumber. He woke with a stretch and a yawn excited for his big day. He whistled a cheerful tune as he headed to the bathroom. After showering and freshening up, Alastor and Azazel came into his hotel room.

"Well today is the big day," Azazel snickered. Alastor stood in the bedroom doorway with his arms folded.

"Don't just stand there. Help him with his tie," he commanded. Azazel helped with Moranvale's tie, giving a nice tight pull at the end.

"By the way, you will be part of tonight's show," Azazel smiled. "Don't worry, it's just for entertainment." He patted Moranvale on the back and walked out of the room. "Don't be long. There is a taxi waiting for you outside. We will meet you at the club later." Moranvale checked himself in the mirror before taking the elevator down to catch the cab.

"Where to bud?" the driver asked.

"To the Bohemian Club for tonight's festivities," he answered. "I hope everything goes as planned."

"I hope so too," the driver snickered. Moranvale glimpsed up at the rear view mirror and felt an eerie chill when he seen his eyes turn as black as coal.

Sandra and Hall paid for a couple of motel rooms with the last little bit of money they had that night. Before they left in the morning Salles wanted to go over the plan with everyone.

"Good morning ladies. How did everyone sleep last night?" Spiked asked when the girls entered their room.

Considering I'm not used to sleeping with a scaly lizard woman, not that great," Sandra replied. Lesa morphed into a likeness of Sandra.

"Would it be better for you if I looked like this?" she mocked her. Sandra stepped back a little.

"No, that's a little too creepy," she replied.

"Well I think the marines prepared me for this," Hall laughed. "You should see some of the girls I was in boot with. Even got to see some girl on girl action on fire watch some nights." Everyone stopped and stared at her. "What? Thirteen weeks with no sex? A girl has to do something." She looked down at the floor her face as red as an apple.

"Okay, back to the important matters," commented Threshold. "Let's go over the plan, Indigo."

"Hold on. I want to hear more about this girl on girl," Spike interrupted.

"Shut up, we don't have time for that," stated Threshold. Hall walked over and sat next to Spike.

"We can save those stories for later," she whispered in his ear.

"Alright, first up is Lesa," Salles explained. "You blend in and scout the area. We won't be too far away. Use the… What is it called again?"

"Bluetooth," Sandra answered.

"Yes, that and Sandra's phone to keep us informed," he continued. "There will be a lot of demons there, but you must keep your head about you. Once you locate the head demon, which is my old friend, you say the end is nigh. Got it?" Lesa nods her head. "I know Badgon is still in there. He can never resist a beautiful woman. The trick is to find the best looking one you can."

"Got it," Lesa replied.

"Ladies, you hang back at the vehicles," he commanded. "Just in case we need to retreat. Men we will be waiting in the trees for the signal. Let's get ready to move out."

The cab travelled down an eerie path through the woods. The trees were decorated for the party. Life like dummies hung from the branches. Moranvale stared out the window in amazement, but he couldn't shake the feeling he was being watched. The taxi finally pulled up to the entrance of the main grounds. Moranvale stepped out of the vehicle.

"Here is a little something for your trouble," he told the driver. He reached into his pocket for some money.

"Don't worry about it," he replied. "The ride is on me, sir." He drove off leaving Moranvale standing with two guards at the gate.

"Come with us, sir," said the first guard.

"We were expecting your arrival, sir," the second guard followed. "We will take you to Alastor." He followed them passed the gate and through the main gathering area.

"Looks like they put together a frightful setting," Moranvale stuttered. A feeling of fear started to settle in. They walked down a long path shadowed by the tall trees until they came upon a small cage. The two guards grabbed Moranvale and he struggled to get free from their grasp.

"What is the meaning of this?!" he yelled. They forced him into the cage. Alastor stepped out of the shadow of the trees in his all black suit. "You! I know you said I will be part of the show, but what is the meaning of this?!"

"Show? There is no show," laughed Alastor. "This is a ritual. Yes, you are a part of it." Moranvale's complexion turned pale white. Alastor paced in front of the cage as he began to explain. "You see, the old witch never said who will have dual rule over both realms. That and Indombe ended the life of *the one that lives amongst the trees*." He stopped and looked at Moranvale with a smile. "You are only needed as a vessel for our leader," he sneered. "We demons cannot enter human bodies without invitation. If our master walks among the living we can come and go as we please. The cleansing ritual will allow that to happen. Tonight that cleansing will commence," Alastor said as he walked away.

"Wait!" Moranvale screamed. "I never asked for this!" Alastor stopped, turned around and glared at him.

"Greed is a one way ticket," he claimed. "What? Did no one teach you? Never trust a man in black." Moranvale's cries for help were silenced by the wind in the trees as Alastor laughed walking away.

Hours have past and the guests have started to arrive. All types of people from all over that are willing to support Moranvale's candidacy. Lesa waited in the shadows of the trees, watching for the perfect victim. She noticed a ginger haired woman in a short light blue gown. Upon seeing the tall, slender woman she knew she was the one. She changed into a copy of the woman and followed her.

"Excuse me miss," she said to her. The woman turned around to see herself staring back at her and fainted out of fright. "Well that was the easy part." She drug the body off to the woods. She rummaged through the woman's purse for an invitation. She found it at the bottom and pulled it out. "Rachele Masden. Hmm that's a nice name. Sorry about this," she apologized. She took her purse when she scrambled to get back to the path before anyone noticed.

"Invitation and identification please," demanded the guard. Lesa pulled both out of the purse and gave them to him. "Enjoy the frightful evening Ms. Madsen." She walked a little ways past the guard before she put the bluetooth in and called Salles.

"I'm in," she whispered. The three warriors leapt through the treetops. They spread out to cover more area.

"I don't see Moranvale," Threshold muttered to himself. "His ass is mine."

"Good, now keep an eye out for Alastor," Salles answered. "You'll know him when you see him." The sun started to set, leaving a pink and purple skyline, while Lesa mingled in the crowd. Fire exploded in front of the stage drawing the attention of the crowd. Four people in black hooded cloaks walked out on stage.

"Guys, I think the party is about to start," she whispered. The cloaked man in the front began to speak into the microphone.

"Wenches and heathens!" he exclaimed. "We are gathered here on this unholy night not to spread joy, but torment!" Elsewhere, Moranvale was being escorted from the cage he was held captive, bound by rope. The two demon guards guided him down the wooded path.

"You all shall be part of the ceremony!" the cloaked man continued. Lesa gazed up in the night sky to see a tornado of shadows swirling above. A man next to her did the same.

"They look so real," he gasped. "I can't even see the projectors." Lesa looked at him with pity and back at the stage.

"Guys, it's starting to look bad out here," she told Salles.

"We do not move until we see Badgon's face, clear?" answered Salles.

"Clear," she replied back. The man looked at her and backed away.

The guards continued to walk Moranvale down the path. He stared at all the, what he thought were, dummies hanging in the trees. Their heads rotated towards him and they all let out a blood curdling screech. The realization of what they were dropped him to his knees in fright. The bodies of all the boys he sentenced to death.

"Get up!" exclaimed the first guard. He pulled Moranvale to his feet.

"Move!" the other guard followed. He pushed him to walk. Moranvale heard whispers all around him as they moved closer and closer to the path's exit.

"Every choice has its consequences," he heard over and over. He frantically looked around, left, right, front and back. The words were absorbed in his mind, driving him mad.

"Make them stop!" he screamed. The guards only pushed him to move faster.

"Stop!" they commanded. They finally reached the end of the path. In front of him hung the young pregnant woman in the tree. Her deathly pale face changed to the one of the old blind crone.

"I never said who will have dual rule!" she laughed. The first guard picked up the long rope that bound Moranvale. He walked towards the beam in front of the stage and threw the rope over it. That signaled the lighting of the pentagram.

"There is one man that is willing to be a sacrifice to better this land!" exclaimed the cloaked man. "Do you let him in?!" The crowd cheered in confirmation. Shadows came down from the whirling mass to take control of two confiding men. They helped the demon guards pull the rope to hoist Moranvale above the fire. The cloaked man continued his rant.

"Right now this man is not worthy of leading this new hell!" he ranted. "After this ritual he will be a worthy eagle king!" The crowd roared in excitement not knowing the true meaning of his words. Moranvale fell on his back as the four men pulled the rope. He slid underneath the old oracle. He hollered in panic as the old oracle laughed and danced above him. Moranvale felt the heat from the burning stones underneath him when he was finally hoisted up. The crowd stared in amazement.

"Man! They went all out for this show!" a woman yelled. The man under the hood finally revealed himself. It was Azazel under the cloak.

"It's not him," Lesa told Salles.

"Well then sniff him out," he commanded. The man from before approached Lesa to talk again. She flicked her tongue out to pick up Alastor's scent.

"Succubus!" he screamed and ran towards the burning pentagram. Azazel and the other three began to chant in aramaic language. A shadow more vast than any other slowly emerged from the flames. Threshold watched the events unfold from his perch in the trees. The demon grew larger and larger, getting closer and closer to Moranvale. He felt a great coldness surge through his body as the shadow started to enter through his feet. Threshold's anger grew and his patience was short.

"If anyone is gonna kill him it's gonna be me!" he roared. He changed into his lion form and jumped from the tree. He flew through the night sky towards Moranvale's dangling body. Grasping the rope, they both swung away from the flames. Threshold bit through the rope sending them crashing to the ground.

"I never thought I would say this but I'm glad to see you, Tobias," Moranvale stated. Threshold came down with a solid clenched paw to the face and knocked him unconscious.

"When I'm done you will wish it wasn't me," he claimed. He grabbed the rope and pulled him towards the woods to lay him off to the side. The immense shadow continued to emerge from the fire. Threshold tried to lunge at the demon but only phased through it.

"Damn it Tobias!" Salles screamed. He signaled for Spike to move in. "Did you target Badgon yet, Lesa?" She continued to sniff the air with her snake like tongue.

"Yes sir," she replied. "Target is acquired."

"Pursue the target," he commanded. "I will join in the battle." The patrons were sent into a panic when the storm of shadows swooped in to take over their bodies. Lesa morphed into her reptilian state and pursued the cloaked figures. She was surrounded by a mob of possessed humans. The tiger and the wolfman came jumping in from the trees to join the fight.

Sandra and Hall were sitting in the Camaro back at the entrance of the woods. Gabriel was lying comfortable in Sandra's lap.

"I hope the guys are alright," she said petting Gabriel.

"I know how you feel," Hall replied. "It's like I wish I could be there and at the same time I'm glad I'm not there." Gabriel sensed there was something wrong. He stood up and dug his claws into Sandra's leg.

"Ow! Shit! What's your problem?!" she complained.

"You have to let me out, now!" he demanded. Sandra said nothing and just opened the door. Gabriel jumped out of the car and ran as fast as he could towards the battle.

The demons that mobbed Lesa kicked and stomped her on the ground. Salles ran over to help her. He bit, slashed and clawed his way through the hoard. After making a path to Lesa, he picked her up and jumped over the remaining possessed. He ran her to the safety of the tree line.

"Where is Badgon?" he asked.

"Third cloaked figure," she faintly muttered. Lesa was weakened and short on breath.

"You rest," he commanded. "There has to be a way to drive a demon out without killing someone. I need my partner back." He left Lesa to track down Alastor. Lesa knew there was a way to do it, but was too weak to follow. Salles bypassed the mass of fallen bodies and demon possessed hoards pursuing the third cloak figure. He ran passed Azazel on the way. Azazel knew he could not fight this battle in Senator Abbott's body, so he decided to hide. He hid in the same place Threshold stashed Moranvale.

"Azazel, untie me," Moranvale whispered startling Azazel. He turned to him and smiled a conniving grin. He crawled over to untie him. They both peered over the hedges to see what's going on. Azazel had the hopes of leading the demon lord towards Moranvale to finish the plan. He closed his eyes to use his demon link to draw the enormous shadow towards them. At the same time Moranvale seen Gabriel run past them and jump over the hedges. Gabriel found Lesa lying there face towards the starry sky. He climbed upon her stomach and laid down to use his angelic powers to heal her. About a minutes time she woke up to find him resting on her.

"You healed me?" she questioned.

"Yes," he answered. "Now go help Indigo." He jumped off her and ran out to the field. Moranvale seen the reptilian woman pop up and dash out of the trees. He then noticed the large demon shadow coming closer to him. He tried to duck behind the bushes to hide.

"Lucifer!" he heard someone yell. The shadow stopped in its tracks. Moranvale looked to see who it was. He was shocked to see that the large voice came from such a small cat. "This ends here!" Gabriel exclaimed. He laid down on the ground and a blinding flash of light arose leaving the little feline's body lifeless. The flash of light drove all the hostless demons, including Lucifer, back to the underworld. Azazel knew that the cleansing was a failure and could only think of one thing to do. He stared at Moranvale for a minute.

"I will make sure our son is well taken care of," he declared. Moranvale looked at him in confusion. Azazel punched through the chest of Senator Abbott and pulled out his heart releasing himself from the vessel.

"No!" Moranvale screamed in terror. He fell backwards on the ground as Azazel entered his body. With his new found powers Azazel took flight as the new eagle king. He looked down upon the people below. In the distance he saw Salles chasing Alastor towards a long wooded path. Lesa not far behind them.

"Marshall!" yelled Salles. Alastor stopped and turned to face him.

"Your friend is no longer with us, dear captain," laughed Alastor.

"You lie, demon!" Salles exclaimed. He began to change form to prepare for battle. "I know you are in there and I'm gonna beat the hell out of you to prove it!" He swiftly lunged at Alastor and grabbed him and threw him against a tree.

"Tisk, tisk, tisk. Oh captain, don't you know I'm stronger than you?" chuckled Alastor. He got up off the ground and changed form too. Throwing the cloak to the side. He swiped his right claw across Salles' cheek drawing blood. "You only held me back from my full potential!" He followed with a left making that side match the right. Salles tried to fight back but he seemed stronger than their last encounter. Lesa drew nearer to the fight, but Azazel had other plans for her. Before she could reach the path, Azazel swooped down and picked her up by the arms.

"I really don't think he needs your help," he laughed. He flew her higher and higher. She looked down to see Spike biting, slashing and ripping the heads of the possessed patrons of the party. What she failed to notice is Threshold in the tree tops again. He pounced from his position and tackled Azazel in mid air. The hit forced him to drop Lesa. She looked up at Moranvale as she was falling, then she morphed into a copy of him. She aimed towards Spike to dive bomb him and get his attention. He didn't see Threshold and Azazel crash into the ground, so he assumed that she was Moranvale. She led him down the path towards Alastor and Salles. Salles was in a weakened state leaning against a tree. Alastor walked up to him and picked him up by the throat.

"You see, captain," Alastor snarled. "The cleansing was supposed to bring our lord here. You messed that up. The ritual also made us lesser demons stronger. You have no chance of winning this." Salles seen Spike, from the corner of his eye, charging at Alastor. He gasped for enough air to speak.

"You may be stronger… but we are a pack…" he choked out. With all the strength he had left, Salles swung his legs to kick him in the stomach. Alastor was forced to drop him in time for Spike to tackle him to the ground. Alastor laid there with the giant wolf on top of him. Teeth showing and drool dripping on his face. Lesa landed behind where Spike had him pinned down. She changed from Moranvale back to the beautiful Rachele Masden.

"Get off me you mutt!" Alastor exclaimed.

"Spike! Hold!" commanded Salles. He was still weak and struggled to crawl towards them. "I know Badgon is still in there. We have to bring him out." Spike did not move even though he had the urge to kill. The drool continued to drip upon his face. Badgon began an attempt to take his body back. His head flopped back and forth as if he was struggling with himself. "Marshall! If you are in there I have something for you! Spike, let him go." he commanded. Against his better judgement, Spike did what he was told. The internal struggle continued, Badgon's head flopped back and forth on the ground. Lesa approached the body when the motion stopped. Badgon's body changed back to human form. He stood up, but who was he actually. His eyes kept blinking back and forth between human and demon. Lesa walked up to the dazed man and a smile came across his face.

"Hello miss," he stuttered. She took him in her arms.

"Marshall, you are the bravest strongest man I know," she told him.

"Get your hands off me you wench!" Alastor exclaimed. She kissed him before he could break free from her embrace.

"Thank you," Badgon whispered faintly. He collapsed to the ground and Alastor was forced to flee the lifeless vessel. Transforming back to his human form Salles collapsed next to his friend.

"What have you done!" he cried in tears.

"I did what you wanted," she replied with a smile.

"Who would have thought that a kiss from a princess would really lead to a happy ending?" Spike laughed.

"Damn it! Now is not the time to joke!" Salles cried. Spike looked towards Lesa for an explanation.

"Relax, he is not dead," she comforted. "I gave him a low dose of my venom. It only slows the heart rate down to cause the appearance of death. It should wear off in a couple of hours."

"I know I'm not the smartest, but even I knew that, captain," chuckled Spike. Salles gave him a blank stare.

"Well don't just stare at each other," Lesa demanded. "Let's get him out of here before they realize he's not dead." Spike lifted Badgon onto his shoulders and started down the wooded path. He already massacred most of the possessed filling the grove with blood and lifeless bodies. They stopped to gaze upon the horrific scene.

"It does look bad, but they forced our hand," Salles said in dismay. "With every success there is sacrifice. They did not die in vain." They each shed one tear before they heard Threshold hit the ground with a thud. "Get him to the car!" he commanded. "I'll help Tobias!"

"You are still weak from Alastor," Lesa commented.

"Just go!" exclaimed Salles. He changed back to his tiger form and ran to Threshold. The lion jumped back to his feet and stopped Salles.

"No!" he yelled. "This is my fight! Go with the others!" Salles was not shocked by his response.

"Are you sure?" he asked.

"Yes! Now go!" he demanded. They stood there side by side. Staring at Azazel in the sky.

"Remember this one thing," he told him. "You cannot control the outcome if you cannot control yourself." He ran to catch up with the others. "You've finally earned my trust, but you still have a lot to learn," Salles said to himself. Azazel landed a few feet away from Threshold.

"I was there," Azazel claimed. "I was the one who killed your family!" His words infuriated Threshold. "The way I pulled your daughter's head off. The snapping sound was beautiful," he laughed. "Yes, and watching your wife's entrails hit the ground. That was a work of art. It's just so sad that the only heir to your name had to rip his own throat out, but orders are orders." Threshold lunged at him out of anger. Azazel took flight to dodge the attack. He swooped down and kicked Threshold in the back knocking him to the ground. The lion punched the ground in frustration. Azazel was just toying with him.

Salles caught up with Spike and Lesa walking up to the Sandra and Hall. They got out of the Camaro in a panic.

"Is everything good? Where is Tobias?!" questioned Sandra.

"Who the hell is this guy?" Hall asked.

"An old friend that had a bad time," Salles replied. "Tobias is busy fighting Moranvale. I'm going back to help." Spike laid Badgon in the back seat of the Camaro.

"Oh come on! Why in my car!" Hall complained. Sandra smiled at her.

"Yours is the only one with a big enough back seat," she chuckled. Hall rolled her eyes at her.

"So you're saying I have a big rear end?" she responded. After putting Badgon in the car, Spike changed back to his human form.

"Wouldn't say big. Just comfortable," he commented. They both scowled at him. "What? Did I say something wrong?"

Salles ran to see how Threshold was handling the situation. When he arrived at the battle ground Threshold was lying on his back beaten and exhausted.

"Calm down and focus!" he yelled from the trees. "Don't let emotions cost you a victory!" Threshold looked around to see where the voice came from, he seen no one.

"Was that the Divine One?" he thought to himself. Taking the advice, he took a few deep breaths and collected his thoughts. He stood up and brushed the dirt from his fur. He surveyed the area then made a break for the surrounding trees.

"Giving up now, Tobias!" Azazel exclaimed. "Just like a cowardly lion! I can't allow you to walk away!" Azazel gave chase not knowing Threshold was at home amongst the trees. A little ways in the dark woods Threshold was perched high in a tree. He was waiting for him to catch up. Azazel flew by tree after tree scouting the ground.

"Here kitty, kitty, kitty!" he mocked him. Threshold jumped from his perch when he flew by. He landed on Azazel's back sending them crashing to the ground. He did not give Azazel a chance to get up. They rolled around in a ground struggle until Threshold pinned him down.

"This is for my wife!" he yelled. He hit Azazel in the face with a right claw. "And my kids!" He followed with a left to the face. He repeated the combination four or five times before he continuously shook him. Azazel's head banged off the ground until he seemed lifeless.

"Enough, Tobias!" Salles yelled creeping up behind him. Moranvale gasped for breath.

"Let me die," he mumbled. "I deserve… it… for…" His eyes rolled back as he breathed his last breath. Salles helped the exhausted lion to his feet. Both battered and bruised they stood eye to eye as they morphed to their human forms.

"There is nothing more we can do here," stated Salles. "Let's go meet with the others. We have a lot to discuss." They headed out of the woods towards to path. Threshold leaned on Salles like a crutch as they headed off into the darkness. Azazel took over the dying eagle king's body.

"You are not dying," he said as he started to crawl. "You cannot repent and expect the Divine One to accept you." He inched his way out of the woods to the grove of bodies. He crawled through the blood stained field, over the disemboweled corpses and decapitated heads. He finally made it to the burning pentagram. "As long as there is an ounce of life left in this body, the fires of hell shall revitalize you." Azazel collapsed next to the fire and began to chant. The flames turned blue, flickered and jumped leaving a life essence in the air. He breathed in that essence before he closed his eyes to rest.

A NEW BEGINNING

Threshold and Salles made their way back to the meeting point. Upon arrival, Sandra ran up and embraced Threshold. He grunted in pain when she squeezed him.

"I'm so sorry," she apologized. "I'm just glad you are alive. You had me worried."

"It's fine," he grunted holding his side. "I just need the cat and a little rest. Where is Gabriel?" Hall and Spike were in their own embrace on the hood of the Camaro.

"He ran off a while ago," Hall answered. "The direction he ran, I assumed he was going to help you guys." Lesa was back in her Rachel Masden persona.

"He did. He healed me then ran off," she commented. "Strange thing is there was a flash of light a little after he left." As she was talking a little gray squirrel jumped down from a tree. It ran towards Threshold and climbed up his pants and rested on his shoulder.

"I'm feeling a little tired now," mumbled Threshold. He then collapsed on the ground.

"Well sacrifices had to be made," said the little squirrel. They were all excited to see that Gabriel came back. "Sorry to inform you of this but the situation was only temporarily delayed. There is more trouble brewing back in Pixima."

"Yes, with Moranvale dead there is no one to rule," Salles responded. Gabriel jumped off Threshold and climbed up on the roof of the Camaro. He got right up in Salles' face.

"No!" he exclaimed. "When Alastor brought him here he left Lilith in charge of the kingdom. I don't mean to cut your celebration short, but she must be put in her place!" Everyone knew the day would come that will separate them, but his words infuriated Sandra and Hall. Enraged, Sandra walked up to the little squirrel.

"What do you mean?!" he yelled at him. "I just found out Tobias is barely even alive and now you are telling me they have to leave!" The little squirrel backed away from the angered woman.

"Calm down!" Hall screamed at her. "We all see your love for him, but you have to see the big picture here!" She walked up to Sandra. "It's not about you and Tobias! It's not about me and Spike! It's not about any us! It's about all of us!" She took her in her arms giving her a comforting embrace. "If it was meant to be it will all work out." Sandra choked back her tears.

"You're right," she sobbed.

"Yes she is right," commented Lesa. "But to get back to Pixima we must first go back to… where I left your friend. I kinda feel bad about that." She stared down at the ground. Salles shook his head in response.

"Let's just get him in the back with the marshall," he commanded. Spike grabbed Threshold's legs and Salles grabbed his arms.

"See, I told you had a bigger rear end," he told Hall as he walked by. Lesa changed back to her Buxton persona before Salles and she walked to the Dodge. Salles was curious why.

"If you can look like anyone you want, why did you change to that?" he asked. She opened the door and sat down. Then he got in the other seat.

"If you want to find the place, I need to know what she knows," she answered. "Just to warn you. If we can get through that way you will be in reptilian territory. They aren't nice people. That's why I left when I had the chance." She started the car and backed out to head down the long dirt road. The others followed with Sandra, alone, bringing up the rear.

Lilith was lounging in her king sized bed with red satin sheets. She rang her servant bell.

"Oh humble servant!" she beckoned. In walked the colored farm boy.

"Yes, my lady?" he answered her call. She gazed at him seductively.

He replied, "As you wish," and started to undress. He climbed into the bed and began to kiss her neck passionately. She forced her way on top of him and began to have her way with the boy. A cold breeze blew through the window letting in a hint of the fall sun.

"Get off me, you foul woman!" yelled the servant as he threw her to the floor. Lilith jumped up from where she landed.

"It is your duty to pleasure me! How dare you defy your queen!" she screamed at him.

He pointed at her and replied, "Because if it wasn't for me, you wouldn't be queen in the first place!" Lilith through her hands up in disgust.

"Oh great!" she complained. "Alastor is back! Don't tell me, you messed up the cleansing and now you're here to annoy me?!"

"Believe me, everything was going according to plan," he stated. "That damn lion just didn't want to die." He turned his back to Lilith and stated, "I never thought three miscreants could be such a pain in the ass." Lilith picked up the farm boy's clothes from the floor.

"Speaking of pain in the ass," she commented. "Why don't you put some clothes on?" She through the garments at him. "Obviously you are not fit to run a kingdom. For now you will be my second in command.

"I made you who you are!" Alastor screamed. "I will not take orders from you!"

"Yes you did, "she smiled. "You made me queen and my subjects expect me to run this place. Not a poor small town farm boy." She strutted towards the bedroom door. "Now put some clothes on," she commanded. She closed the door behind her and Alastor stood there naked holding the garments.

The next day at the Abbott home, Gretchen was watching her soap opera. She wondered why her husband had not come home yet. Her show just ended and the twelve o'clock news was about to start. She got up to start some cleaning when she heard the reporter come on the television.

"Tragic events unfolded last night at the Bohemian Club in California," he stated. "A small terrorist group invaded the presidential candidate, Edward Moranvale's fundraiser resulting in the loss of many lives. Amongst the lives lost was Washington's own Senator Clint Abbott. Let's go to an earlier interview with the surviving Edward Moranvale." Gretchen dropped to her knees in tears. She thought to herself, *"How can something so innocent turn so tragic?"*

"The events that happened here last night only proves Senator Abbott was right," claimed Azazel. "I support his gun confiscation bill a hundred percent. If I win this election I will do everything in my power to see that bill will become a law. I will also make sure the individuals responsible for this massacre will be found and severely punished." Gretchen was distraught and confused. Her mind raced with so many worries. *"I'm pregnant and alone. I can't raise a child like this. Why has this happened? Lord, please give me an answer."* The doorbell suddenly rang, but Gretchen couldn't bring herself to answer it. She sat there staring at the television. The doorbell rang again. She still did not move. The door slowly creaked open.

"Hello? Mrs. Abbott? Is everything okay?" said a man's voice. She turned to see who was in her house. She stood up and ran to Azazel. He embraced her to ease her pain. "You are not alone in this," he comforted her. "I will be here to make sure you and the baby are well taken care of." Gretchen cried soaking his chest in tears.

They drove all night to get back to the Denver Airport. Due to the situation Salles thought it would be best for Badgon and Threshold to ride with him. Badgon was just waking up from his long, well needed, rest.

"Where the hell am I?" he whispered. He snapped awake when he realized who he was next to. "Threshold! Escaped convict!" he exclaimed. "Have to inform the captain!" He went to leave but realized he was stuck in a car. He was still groggy from the venom when he reached for the door handle.

"Lesa, lock the doors," commanded Salles. "Marshall! Calm down! Everything is alright. Tobias is one of us." Badgon was befuddled about the situation. His memories were broken between instances. "What all do you remember?" he asked.

"Only bits and pieces, sir," he answered. "I remember fighting you, but it was like I couldn't control myself. Most of all I remember a kiss from the most beautiful woman I ever seen. Where is she?" Salles looked at Lesa with a smile.

"Well… she is here, but I don't think you will like what you see," he chuckled.

"Now why would you say that, sir?" Badgon asked. They finally arrived at the airport.

"It's a long story," Salles answered. "You don't have to call me sir. We don't work for Moranvale anymore," he told Badgon. He stepped out of the car.

"Time to wake up, Tobias!" Lesa yelled. "Time to go home!" Threshold was startled awake and looked to see where they were. He noticed the horse statue.

"Buxton is gonna kill me," he mumbled to himself. He unlocked the door and stepped out. Badgon crawled over to Threshold's side to get out. "Why don't you get out your side?" he asked him.

"Honestly? I don't know how," he answered. The sun was setting as they went to enter the underground chamber.

Buxton was sitting on the stairs looking over the documents she found. She heard the chamber door open. She closed the folder and stood up fast. She dropped the old candy bar she got from a vending machine she found. Threshold lead the others down the stairs to the place they discovered. When he got to the bottom Buxton ran up and slapped him.

"Why did you leave me here?!" she yelled at him. "Before he could answer, Lesa walked up behind him.

"It's not his fault," she stated.

"What the hell?" Buxton gawked. She was shocked to be staring at herself. Threshold rubbed his cheek to sooth the sting.

"I'm Lesa Elza of the Oasis," she explained. Buxton circled her staring in astonishment.

"That doesn't explain why you look like me," she stated. Badgon came walking down the stairs behind them.

"It's kinda hard to explain, so I guess I can show you," she replied. She morphed into her reptilian form. Buxton and Badgon both jumped back in fear.

"Wait, relax!" Salles exclaimed. "If it wasn't for her we wouldn't be here right now and you would still be eating those old chocolate bars!" He looked at all the wrappers on the ground.

"Well I had no choice at the moment," she muttered. She opened her lab coat and looked down. "I think I gained a little weight."

"Anyway," Salles interrupted. "Tobias said there should be a way back to Pixima here. Did you find anything?"

"In fact I have," she answered. She handed him the documents she found. "You see, my theory was correct. This whole place was built for interdimensional travel using pressure systems and magnetism. Those papers state that the experiment was a success. The project was abandoned though and Dr. Martin Cosgrove disappeared after his return from the other side."

"Yea," Lesa shamefully replied. "That was me that returned. He died in the Oasis. The others like me are intolerant of outsiders and tend to get a little violent. I had to escape from there. You were my only way out of this dungeon. I'm sorry."

"Don't tell me you're the one who kissed me?" questioned Badgon. Lesa changed into her tall, ginger, Rachel Masden persona and looked at him.

"Yes it was me that saved your life," she responded.

"Damn cold blood," he mumbled. "Was the best kiss I ever had though."

"Okay! Enough of this!" Salles demanded. "We have more pressing matters at hand. Like how does this thing work. The Oasis is a long ways away from Branville."

"It's actually a complex process put into simplicity," Buxton answered.

"Well then simplify it!" he demanded.

"Well in simple terms, there is an office on the first floor of both buildings. At each desk there is a lever. One controls temperatures and air pressure and the other controls magnetism. First person pulls one and when the pressure is at or above a certain degree the other uses the magnets to pull the molecules apart. It's gonna take all three of us girls to make sure everything goes right."

"I guess everyone should say their goodbyes and get ready for this," Salles said. "I'm truly sorry for the hell you had to endure during this mishap," he apologized. He shook her hand and pulled her in for a hug. Spike and Hall came face to face and gazed into each other's eyes. No words could express the feelings they had at the moment, so Spike leaned in for a goodbye kiss.

"Please don't let this be goodbye," Hall whispered. Her eyes still closed and her arms around his neck.

"Just think of it as a see you later," Spike replied. "I will see you when it's all done and over." He lifted her by the hips and gave her one last goodbye kiss.

Things were a little more awkward between Threshold and Sandra. He slowly walked up to her in a shy manner.

"I know this has been a hell of an endeavor we have been through. I can't help but to feel that I have grown attached to you," he confessed. "I feel it is too soon to say love but you remind me so much of Estella that I can't resist these feelings I have." He leaned in for a kiss and Sandra just pulled away.

"That was a touching speech you gave there, but I think the one that needs to hear it is behind me," smiled Lesa. She stepped to the side, revealing the real Sandra.

"I understand how you feel," she sobbed. Tears swelled in her eyes. "Just promise me that we will meet again." She put her arms around his waist and he embraced her back.

"Through life or death, I shall return to you," he promised.

"Okay! Let's fire this thing up and head home boys!" Spike blurted out.

"Yes," Hall followed. "I will take the left building. Sandra, you take the right."

"How will we know what to do and when?" questioned Sandra.

"Well that's easy," Buxton answered. "On the desks by the switches are intercoms. There is also one out here by the platform. That way the one out here can tell the ones inside to flip the switches."

"Okay! To our stations!" Hall exclaimed. Sandra nodded in acceptance and they both ran to their assigned buildings. When Hall made it to the desk she said, "On post," over the intercom.

"Good," Buxton replied over the com. "Sandra are you there?" It was silent for a minute. She tried again, "Sandra?"

"Okay, I'm in," she finally answered. "Took me a minute to find it. Had to follow the trail of candy bar wrappers."

"Yea… sorry about that," Buxton apologized. "Jeanette, you're up first." Hall lifted up on the switch. Scorching hot winds came from the left side of the room and icy winds from the right colliding on the platform in the center. The pressure was building in the sealed room. When the clouds of the jet stream started to form, Buxton got on the com. Her hair and lab coat flopped fiercely in the winds. "Okay! Your turn Sandra!" She then pulled her switch and four rods holding the strongest neodymium magnets angled around the clouds. The clouds began to separate, pulling towards the magnets. The separation opened the way to the Oasis.

"Well it's time to take back the kingdom!" Threshold yelled in the wind.

"Yes, but the Oasis is a journey's away to Branville!" Salles replied.

"And reptilians aren't nice people!" commented Lesa.

"But it's a journey we must endure!" Spike exclaimed.

"I don't know how we got here, but let's just go home!" Badgon yelled. All five of them walked through the opened gate to begin their journey back to Branville. Buxton got on the intercom to give the shutdown instructions.

"Okay ladies!" she yelled. "The key to shutting this down is to shut off magnets first!" Sandra tried to pull her lever down first but it wouldn't budge. Hall thought she had enough time enough time to get it done, so she pulled her lever. The clouds dissipated leaving no evidence of the portal behind. "Looks like everything is shut down. Guess we can leave now," she told them. Hall came out of the building, but Sandra was still trying to shut down the magnets. She finally gave up and came out too.

"Now that this is all over, what are we going to do?" asked Sandra. "It's not like we can just go home. I mean I have no job to go back too."

"Yea and we are basically on the run," Hall added. "They consider me a deserter and you stole that van."

"That is a valid point you have," Buxton answered. "I'm not sure what we should do yet." They headed towards the stairs to exit the facility.

"I don't know about you guys but I need a drink," sighed Hall.

"Good idea," Sandra responded. "I did see a bar not too far away. Maybe we can figure out what's next after we relax a bit." Buxton and Hall exited the top of the stairs to go outside. Sandra stopped and looked at the platform one last time. "Good luck, Tobias," she muttered before she left. When they closed up the entrance a leaf appeared and drifted upon the platform.

Lilith and Alastor argued for awhile before they decided to speak with the old oracle.

"I am the queen so let me do the talking," Lilith commanded. They again made the journey down the dark stairwell.

"And if I don't comply?" questioned Alastor.

"Then I will have you beheaded!" she exclaimed. The tall blonde woman burst through the witch's door. The slamming of the door did not startle the old woman. She continued to stare into her cauldron with her blind eyes.

"Yes your majesty. Your coming has been foreseen," she welcomed them.

"If you seen us coming, woman, then tell me why we are here," Lilith demanded. The oracle continued gazing into the pot. Her dark hood still on to cover her decrepit face.

"You seek the answers that were already told," she replied. "Do you not have dual rule over both realms?" she asked.

"No," Alastor answered. Lilith stuck the back of her hand in his face to silence him.

"Moranvale is dead and so is Azazel," claimed Lilith. The oracle laughed in response.

"Defeat does not mean death," she stated. "Shear determination to survive is the victory in defeat. I see you are here to see what is to come."

"Yes, show us," Lilith demanded. The oracle beckoned for Lilith.

"Come, come see for yourself," she answered. Lilith approached the old crone slowly and stood next to the old woman.

"I see nothing but this disgusting liquid!" she exclaimed.

"The eyes cannot see," claimed the oracle. "The answers are only revealed to an open mind. Take my hand." Lilith took the old woman's hand in hers. "Do you see it?" she asked.

"Yes," she replied. "I see it all. I see Moranvale in front of a huge crowd. There are signs that say *LET'S MAKE AMERICA GREAT AGAIN!*"

"What else is there?" asked the oracle.

"I only hear words," she answered. "They say, wars shall be won in the name of kingdom come. Rivalries will emerge along with alliances. Now I see something." Lilith fell silent and she let go of the oracle's hand. Her face turned ghostly pale. She said nothing as she gave the crown to Alastor and left the room. The old crone removed her hood and faced Alastor.

"Even though hands have changed, your fate still remains the same!" she laughed. Alastor was confused and chased after Lilith. He heard the old woman laughing and laughing as he disappeared into the shadows of the stairs.

About the Author

Craig Temple was born in the small town of Muncy, Pennsylvania and the youngest of three kids. Being born into a military family, staying in that town was not an option. When he was in second grade he had to move to Philadelphia, Pennsylvania for a year and a half and then to Virginia Beach, Virginia where he grew up and graduated high school. After graduation Craig decided to join the Marine Corps only to be sent home with a shoulder injury. Throughout his life Craig has made many attempts to make something out of himself. From songwriting to becoming a certified bail enforcement agent. He decided to stick with what he is good at. That is cooking, writing and making people think.

About the Book

After King Edward Moranvale of the land of Pixima made a deal with the Underworld Council, the Demon Wars struck the land. He promised the souls of the lion race in exchange for more power. The entire race was wiped out except for one, Tobias Threshold. Out of rage for the loss of his family he tried to kill the king. Only to be thrown in the dungeon. After his assisted escape he was chased through the Jungles of Pixima. He fell upon a rift that lead to Washington D.C. Lost and alone, he unwillingly lead the demons to this new world. Now will Threshold and a few others be able to save both Pixima and America from being taken over? This is bad meets evil. Who will win?